Olena's Calling

Chris Vetterli

To Venessa
Enjoy!
Chris Vetterli

First Edition

Edited by: Chris Vetterli
Cover image and design by: Marcelle Adam

ISBN: 978-1-9992271-0-4 (Book)
978-1-9992271-1-1 (PDF)
978-1-9992271-2-8 (eBook)
978-1-9992271-3-5 (Audiobook mp3)

Printed and bound in Canada by

Rapido Livres Books
Montreal, QC

Acknowledgements

A big thank you to Mark Boyko, Allison Hanes, Damian Inwood, Joanne Maltby, Char Miller, and Nancy Sikich for reading this book in its various stages of development, and for offering me your comments and critiques. Your insights helped me to flesh out the bits and your support confirmed that the writing wasn't too bad for a first-time novelist.

Also a big thank you to Marcelle Adam for reading the book and providing feedback, and especially for her creativity in designing the cover and cover image.

A special big, big thank you to Mike and Danielle Vetterli who gave me some great feedback, and who put up with my virtual obsession while writing this book when I probably should have been doing other things.

Thank you to all the characters and situations that popped into my brain as I was writing this story, which is first and foremost a work of fiction. There are, however, some elements on their own or mixed together, arising from real people, real events, real memories, but there are very few living people who would recognize them. One such person is my sister, Marta Romana Nawalkowsky Boyko, to whom this long short story is dedicated.

Happy 75th Birthday, Marti.   Love, Chris.

Chapters

Appendix

Chapter 1

Olena's Funeral 2004

It's Happened

On Tuesday evening, I cleaned up after dinner, fed my cat, and curled up with him on my living room sofa. At last, I could put my feet up and read the book that had been recommended weeks ago but that gathered dust on my coffee table instead. I felt relaxed for the first time in days and grateful for the A/C that circulated cool air through my south-facing apartment.

Partway into Chapter Two, my Blackberry chimed. I checked its call display, hoping it was a call I could ignore, but instead, I let out a slow sigh. The call was coming in from Olena's number and I knew what it was about.

I scooted the cat off my neck, put down the book, and sat up at attention. Answering the call, I heard Peter's voice croak on the other end, "Hello, Nicole?"

He choked up and began to cry. I spoke instead, giving him a chance to settle and get going again.

"It's ok, Peter, you don't have to say it. I'll come as soon as I can. I'll call Karolina, ok? Is Marko with you?"

Peter took a moment to recover and spoke with a sad, exhausted tone. He told me that Marko arrived a few days ago, but now he'd gone out somewhere and Peter wasn't sure when he'd be back. That bastard never stuck around when something went wrong.

"Does Elizabeth know yet?" I asked.

Peter answered, "I don't think so. Could you call her for me, please? Marko should call her himself, but you know how that could go."

"Sure, I'll do that," I said. "You have enough on your hands. What should I tell her?"

Olena was Peter and Marko's mother, and she had died late last night. Through a gossamer thread of relation, she was the person who came the closest to being my real aunt and I always thought of her as such. I loved her as if we had sprouted from the same branch instead of only being grafted there.

She drifted off in the familiar surroundings of her apartment in which she had lived for over fifty years. Visitations at the funeral home were set for Wednesday and Thursday. Her funeral mass at the Catholic Church would be held on Friday, followed by her burial on Mount Royal and a wake at a local restaurant. That's all Peter could tell me at that moment.

Olena had objected to us planning a "Celebration of Life" and requested no such thing. It seemed very odd to her that the person being celebrated was the only one who couldn't attend. A dinner at Nektarios' restaurant would be fine but we were not to drag it out and, god forbid, display any pictures of her. She promised a good haunting if we did.

I called my sister Karolina to give her the news. Leaving a voicemail, I started, "Hi Karolina, it's me, Nicole. There's been a tragedy..."

Then I called Elizabeth, picking up the slack for Marko. I told her what had happened and asked if I could hitch a ride with her up the 401.

All of us would be packing tonight and making our way to Montreal as quickly as possible. In the morning I would take the GO Express bus from Hamilton to meet Elizabeth and drive with her from Toronto, and Karolina would take the train from Ottawa. First I had to ask Nancy-next-door to take care of my cat again. I was sure she wouldn't mind.

Montreal

Elizabeth gave us a ride from St. Michael's church in the east end of Montreal to the cemetery on Mount Royal on a cool and rainy late summer Friday afternoon. The sky was dark and foreboding, and weeping for our loss. The streets were slick with oil residue from forty-seven previous days of hot, dry weather, and the old car tried its best to hold together as it skittered over potholes on nearly balding tires. There was quite a bit of cross-town traffic with families snaking their way to the Autoroute travelling north to the Laurentians for the weekend. They were headed for some fun, but we were not.

The car windows were rolled up against the rain and were steaming up from the warmth of our bodies huddled inside. We were parts of a small distance-fractured family and Olena brought us together even after death. She was the central grapevine of our family, the one who kept everyone informed and connected. Throughout the years, Olena called with updates about who was doing what, and as our family members moved further apart from each other over time, Olena's reports became more important to keep us unified in some way. Now we weren't sure who would step up to fill the role of the person who tied us all together.

Sitting in the back seat of the old Volvo, crushed between Karolina and her huge husband, I remembered the time when Elizabeth and my cousin Marko came to visit us in Hamilton. Their relationship was on-again and off-again, an easy, breezy affair that endured through gaps in time and place. Marko was sitting beside her again in the front seat.

Trying to cut the silence in the car, I recounted a little snippet of a small event.

"Elizabeth? Do you remember when you and Marko came to visit us in Hamilton? You gave my mom those delicious pies…the ones you baked…the ones you kind of sat on."

Karolina jabbed me in the ribs with her elbow, admonishing sharply, "Nicole!" She gave me a stink-eye that Elizabeth caught in her rearview mirror, but she just laughed and played right along.

Handing over the pies, Elizabeth had admitted with a laugh and a slight shrug of her shoulders to having fallen back on them by accident.

"Oh yeah, I remember! Your mom tried so hard to be gracious when I gave her those smashed things. Wow, I wish you hadn't remembered that, Nicole. But I'm just really glad I didn't leave an imprint of my bum!" Elizabeth exclaimed.

Mount Royal

By the time we got to the cemetery parking lot on Mount Royal, the rain had stopped. We climbed out of the car and walked a fair distance to the burial site. Along the way, water droplets continued to fall from gorgeous old oak and maple trees. Their branches sagged from the weight of their rain-soaked leaves, creating a verdant tunnel leading us to our destination.

The hole had already been dug, ready to receive the casket containing the remains of the person who had hugged us, fed us, and made us feel loved. As we listened to the priest say his words of prayer and to the women and men who sang the sad, solemn songs of tribute and sorrow, I noticed an older gentleman standing alone apart from us over to my left, trying to hide behind a tree whose trunk was unfortunately too thin to be of much use as a disguise. He was tilting a little to his left and right as if he had an uncomfortable stitch in his side.

We were all sniffling and tearing up, but this man was in full-blown, unconstrainable distress. He probably would have howled like a wounded animal if he'd thought of it, but instead he cried and blew his nose and wiped his tears with a large handkerchief, and made loud child-like sobbing, schnuffling sounds.

He stood apart from us, perhaps because he wasn't family, probably because he was embarrassed for not concealing his emotions at all. He only looked straight ahead and didn't try to engage with any of us.

I didn't notice him when we were at the church. There weren't very many people there and I surely would have heard him crying. He didn't seem to have come with anyone so he must have driven up to the cemetery all by himself.

I didn't know who the man was but, clearly, the person in that box meant everything to him.

When Olena's burial site ceremony ended, we lingered a little, tossing some lovely red poppies onto the lid of her coffin. They were her favourite. Then Karolina said, "Come on, Nicole, the priest looks like he wants to go home. Let's go." We shook his hand and thanked him, and then we turned to walk back to the car.

The crying man had already disappeared.

Chapter 2

In the Old Country 1865–1940

Zustrich

Years ago in its beginning, the encampment in the clearing had no name, but as it grew in a wild swath of birch forest, the inhabitants took to calling it "Zustrich", which simply meant "meeting point".

Being on the ancient Varangian trade route from the Baltic Sea to the Black Sea, many people travelled through Zustrich heading south, and some of them travelled back through again, heading north to their homes. Zustrich acquired a variety of people who settled there over time because the area was beautiful and, most of the time, it was far from danger.

As Zustrich grew, it became known as a place that welcomed those who added some value to the community through skill, brains, or brawn. It was also a place that readily encouraged others of lesser quality to simply pass through, although occasionally their dim-witted or mean-spirited essence was left behind in dark corners. And sometimes from that essence, ugly spawn were born.

Wanted: Warriors

Marauding hordes were pillaging their way through the countryside and had to be stopped before all would be lost. The local rag-tag forces were unorganized collections of willing fighters who were high on aspirations but low on tactical training and weaponry use. They were skilled at using pitchforks and scythes on their farms but not in hand-to-hand combat against the experienced and merciless invaders. They needed more trained soldiers desperately.

Zustrich's de facto mayor sent a communiqué to allies in the north, and reinforcements soon made their way south. MacAntin the Brute was one of them. He was a proud, mighty Scottish warrior who took up the call, leading a band of like-minded men, seeking great honour and fortune as paid mercenaries. But it took them too long to complete their journey, having promptly gotten lost in the untamed forests on the mainland. By the time they arrived in Zustrich from Scotland, ready and anxious to join the battles, the hordes had already passed on through and there was no fight to be had.

Instead, MacAntin and his men found that the small and peaceful settlement of Zustrich had largely been spared any disruption and brutality, and seemed like the perfect place to rest. The inhabitants took one look at them and tried to convince them to stay, having observed their aura of bravery and brashness. They were the first of their type to arrive and would be useful to fill Zustrich's gap in protection and security, although the urgency had subsided in the meantime.

Staying longer than they had ever intended, they picked up some of the local language and they felt welcomed into the burgeoning society. They came as wandering assets and injected their skills of observation, planning, and execution into the mix of abilities of the inhabitants. They were lauded enough to make them feel appreciated. And so, MacAntin and his men decided to stay in Zustrich permanently, integrating successfully. MacAntin married and had children, who later had children and grandchildren of their own. His gravestone is still there, high on a knoll, and keeping watch.

Wanted: Adventure

Three generations after MacAntin arrived, Zustrich was graced by the arrival of a benevolent, educated, wealthy traveller named Lilianna Mudra-Baba who was way ahead of her time. She was fluent in reading, writing, mathematics, and the arts. She wore pants. She wanted no children. She craved adventure.

Lilianna's husband, Ihor Durnay-Pahn (whose last name she refused to take), was heading out on another trade run and would be gone for at least two months. She insisted on joining him this time to experience the wild excitement of an unpredictable journey, as he had always described them before.

Ihor could kick himself for not thinking ahead. He thought she would enjoy hearing his tall tales, as the journeys were nothing like how he had described them. Now she insisted on going with him because it wasn't fair that he should have all the fun and glory. He tried to talk her out of it without admitting his fabrications, but she was already packed and impatiently ready. Ihor was sure that if he gave in just this once and she saw what it was really like, she would never bother him to come again. She might never believe him about anything again either.

Soon Lilianna regretted her insistence, but it was too late to turn back. To her great disappointment, their journey proceeded without incident, without moments of surprise, without unexpected delights. Their long trek following the old route beside fast-flowing rivers and through wide, arable valleys required much effort but offered little reward.

Coming upon Zustrich, she and Ihor planned to stay for only a few days to rest and reprovision before continuing on.

This was where the unpredictable finally happened.

Entering Zustrich's drinking establishment, they chose the wrong table, not knowing the preferences of the locals. Worse yet, Ihor chose the unofficially reserved seat of Giant Bogdan who took great exception to the intrusion. Giant Bogdan was insane, he was unpredictable, and his four foot ten frame was always given a wide berth by the wise.

Too late, Lilianna spied the jagged knife in Giant Bogdan's raised hand as he approached Ihor from behind. In an instant, he lashed out, slashing Ihor on the neck. Ihor slumped to the floor, bleeding out quickly from the long, deep gash. He had no last words beyond a gurgle of blood in his mouth.

Lilianna knew she could not help him and knew she would be next. Running out into the street, she was surrounded by a group of women who had heard the yelling of the men inside, holding Giant Bogdan to account for his crime, yet again. The women were always on alert to help those who were escaping.

Carried away on a wave of generosity, protection, and compassion, and recovering in the safety of their shelter, Lilianna felt she owed the women something in return. Over several late night discussions, Lilianna discovered that none of them had ever left Zustrich and none of them had ever seriously contemplated exerting independence or embarking on an adventure of any sort.

The Academy

Having been brought up in a rarefied aristocratic society where, in addition to having money and power, women enjoyed equal treatment, opportunities, and responsibilities, Lilianna was unaccustomed to accepting limitations or compromises. But the more she moved around in the world, the more she came to realize that this was not the case for most people, particularly women.

She believed she could help the women of Zustrich and its surrounding area. She believed that educated women were the keys to a thriving society, and, at least, they deserved to broaden their horizons as payback for all the work they were expected to do. She believed that in return for having lived a life of privileges, she could afford to give something back.

After a proper burial for Ihor, Lilianna made up her mind to stay in Zustrich for as long as it would take to establish an academy, the likes of which had never been seen there. She sent dispatches back to her estate, which had been left in good hands during their absence, and she travelled back periodically to check on the staff and the property.

But her main concern was devising ways for her students to experience a wider world through books and teachings and experimentations, and to become aware of more choices for their lives and ambitions.

The women were very excited and grateful for the opportunity, but some of the men were wary of the change at first. They felt that they also could benefit from an academy like this and railed against the unfairness. Some were worried about the implications, for them, if all the women chose adventure and left the town. Lilianna tried to assure them that although some might leave, the resulting equalization would raise the standard of living for all. Still, there were grumblings.

Lilianna forged on and founded the *Mudra-Baba Academy of Learning and Adventure,* a private girls' school that drew in young women from near and far. When the young men realized this meant that new and interesting young women would be coming to live in Zustrich, they encouraged their fathers to stop opposing and to damn well show some support for the idea.

Ambassadors

Danusia's parents heard about the academy from ambassadors dispatched by Lilianna. In a group of three for safety, they thundered into the centres of villages and towns on horseback, catching people's attention by their unusual and unexpected appearance.

The trio wore jewel-toned red, green, or blue satin Sharovary pants and thigh-length, grey felt jackets with soft, white rabbit fur collars. Their long, flowing hair trailed out behind them as they rode. Often mistaken for the three Furies of ancient Greek mythology, their mission was not one of vengeance. There was no better way to advertise an academy of learning and adventure for girls than to send an all-female competent team to make the right impression.

The horseback Furies dismounted from their tired horses and first sought out fresh water for them and gave them oats from their saddlebags. Naturally, a crowd gathered around them out of pure curiosity. Relieved that they were not there to cause any harm, the citizens were eager to hear why they had come.

Danusia's parents listened intently, watched closely, and determined quickly that the academy would provide a great opportunity for Danusia to get out from near-slave labour on the collective farm where they lived. At the very least, by leaving, she would have a better chance to find a suitable husband rather than any of the lunk-heads who made up her area's pack of wild and education-resistant young men.

Her parents signed the enrollment forms handed out by the Furies, eager to take advantage of the unexpected opportunity immediately, to not miss the chance. Not this time. They'd been burned before by putting off decisions; losing out on buying the best milking cow, missing a deadline to buy a small piece of property, arriving too late to start a good job.

They did not know how it would all turn out, but they were captivated by the Ambassador Furies' enthusiasm and trusted what they described about the school and its purpose. Even if Danusia would only become one of them, she would be in a better position in the future than she was now.

Irony of Intention

As a bewildered Danusia settled into her new temporary home, she wondered how all this had happened. It seemed that Lilianna had thought of everything in advance—the enticements, the transport, the boarding arrangements, and the curriculum.

Everything, except how the girls themselves might feel after being ripped from their surroundings for "their own good".

Lilianna had a head for business and a penchant for educating but having no children of her own, her new students would be, ironically, teaching *her* something about the breadth of human nature. In the beginning, she simply expected the girls to be as resilient and adventurous as she was. In time, she learned that young women stood at different points on the continuum of strength, grace, caution, and decisiveness. Nothing about humans was simple.

Not Home

Boarding with a family whose father, Taras, sold beets and potatoes at the market, Danusia was angry and upset about being sent away from home. She hadn't done anything wrong. She hadn't been given any warning. She wasn't even asked if she wanted to go to this academy.

One minute she was minding her own business picking apples in the orchard. The next minute she was on the back of a truck with two other girls who were not even her friends. She hadn't seen the horseback Furies and only heard about them from the other girls, without the benefit of being captivated by their strength and beauty.

Sitting on the edge of her sleeping spot, in a corner shared with Taras' children, she felt the abyss-like depths of homesickness, an embarrassing weakness that doubled her anger towards her parents. The last image of their resolute, dispassionate faces seared her eyeballs as they stood at the side of the rough, rutted road watching her ride away. Danusia felt her heart harden, and she decided that since they didn't want her anymore, she did not want to speak to them ever again.

In order to look strong and confident in their decision, Danusia's parents sent her away without discussion. They had no practise at this, no guidance from Lilianna on how to let go, and no time to learn. They only knew that their quivering voices would give away their apprehension. They were sure that Danusia would understand eventually, especially if she were taken under the wing of an Ambassador Fury or even Lilianna herself. And so, they chose a tough way, not the best way, to say goodbye.

Unbeknownst to Danusia, in the night of the day she left, her parents cried themselves to sleep, having held in their emotions stoically all day. They did not bear the leaving of their child well. They had the best of intentions, calculated too swiftly. They had always wanted her to have the freedom to grow and fly, and when the Furies handed them the chance, they scooped it up eagerly together, not quite believing their luck.

Now in their quiet home with false echoes of Danusia's voice and where phantom footsteps fell, they were struck with the realization that she might never return.

Danusia had misread their intent entirely.

First Encounter

For most people, September seemed like the rightful start of the year. After a decent break and time for relaxation, with a welcome cooling of the hot summer air, it was the time when routines, broken over the summer, became re-established. To the relief of their parents, children started school again. While many of them were excited to see who would be in their class and who would be new arrivals, most marched back reluctantly.

Mykola had lived in Zustrich his whole life, as had his parents and grandparents before him, all descendants of MacAntin the Brute. Mykola knew of MacAntin's near mythical status as the hero who protected Zustrich, and Mykola's family took great pride in sharing his bloodline, but Mykola felt no leanings towards warring or fighting at all. He was more interested in common boyhood pursuits, like jumping into the lake for a brisk swim or building tree forts in the forest. But lately, his interest and curiosity had turned to the girls of his village.

Mykola was on his way to school where he would begin his tenth-year class. He and his friends had walked this route so many times before; sometimes when he got to the front entrance, it surprised him. Nothing interesting ever happened to shake him out of his morning fog.

But today was different.

"Who is *that*?" he whistled to his friend.

The beautiful, graceful Danusia caught Mykola's attention as she made her way to her first day at the academy. She looked different from the girls he already knew, somehow more confident and older than her age. By the time she turned the corner away from Mykola's route, continuing on to her own school, she knew she had an admirer, but she pretended not to care.

Over the next few days, Mykola dared to catch her attention by riding past her on a borrowed bicycle without holding the handlebars. Another time he caught up from behind her and sheltered her from a downpour with his big, black umbrella until a wind gust blew it inside out.

Every morning on the way to school, Mykola would try to come up with a new antic. But Danusia played it cool as he continued to try to make her notice him. Finally one day, she gave him a little nudge that signalled that she liked him. After school she was going to the nearby forest to hunt for wild mushrooms. She asked if he would join her.

Mushroom Heaven

She boasted that she was an expert in finding the perfect mushrooms that were safe to eat, but she made him taste one that her grandmother had warned was hallucinogenic. Together they entered another world, sometimes trance-like, sometimes euphoric, always better than real life and hard to describe afterwards.

Mykola admitted to Danusia that these crazy mushrooms were the ones he liked best, but he liked her even more. They continued their visits to the forest throughout that fall, until the smell of snow was in the air, stealthily disappearing for hours only often enough not to be suspected.

Sometimes they ate the mushrooms of "grandmother's warning" that Danusia had carefully cleaned, dried, and stored in a small glass jar. Sometimes they just enjoyed being together in a clear and sober state. And almost all of those times, in a private, cozy make-shift hut they had built together from broken branches and pine boughs, they kissed and shared each other while falling deeper in love.

Mushroom Hell

The family was just finishing up dinner on a Monday night when there was a loud and urgent knocking on the front door. Mykola's father, Stefan, opened it and faced Taras, the large man who he knew from the village market. Taras was upset and red in the face, and he blurted out his reason for coming.

Danusia had been put in his charge while she went to school at the academy, and she and Mykola had been up to no good, sneaking around for months. Now, of course, how could it be any other way? She was pregnant.

"You, Mykola. You are the one! " blustered Taras.

Neither Mykola nor Danusia had given any thought to the potential, inevitable, guaranteed results of their hallucinogenic trysts, but now there was no getting around it.

Taras continued to bellow. A new life was being created and someone had to be accountable for it. Taras was angry and embarrassed that this happened on his watch, and he wondered how he would ever be trusted to house another boarder from the school in the future. Most of all, Taras wanted to make sure that he himself would not be suspected. He knew how rumours flew. It was time for Mykola to grow up and take responsibility.

There was yelling.

There was oy-yoying.

The peaceful evening turned sour and difficult with the sounds and sights of Taras and Mykola's parents arguing, pouring accusations onto the floor and lighting a match.

At first, poor naïve Mykola was completely baffled. He had no real knowledge of his power to create life, at least not before marriage. They had always been told that babies come after marriage, because of marriage, not before or without it.

Mykola needed to run and fast, but hefty Taras was blocking the door. He shifted only far enough to let Mykola squeak through the crack between him and the doorframe, taking some satisfaction from seeing Mykola wince as he rubbed up hard against the wood.

Scraping past Taras, Mykola took off for the birch forest that encircled the village. As if on purpose, hundreds of newly sprouted mushrooms taunted his every step.

Up in the trees, an owl hooted, "You-you. You Fool... You-you. You Fool."

After spending some anxious time wandering around the forest alone, he went to see his grandfather because Old Dido was removed from the hysteria over in a small cottage of his own. He was always glad to see Mykola, but Mykola only came when he had a problem to work through. Old Dido sat and listened, and divulged that these matters were not as uncommon as many people thought. He advised that Mykola and Danusia should marry soon, and that no one in Zustrich would suspect anything unusual. Young love was rash and impetuous, plain and simple.

This was a lot to take in. Mykola thought it over, took a deep breath, and returned to his home the next morning with some trepidation, to discuss the situation with his parents. They'd had some time to absorb yesterday's news and as they talked, they seemed much calmer than he expected.

They didn't tell him, and he didn't guess, that he was the result of a similar situation.

Lilianna's Reaction

Danusia's feeling of denial slowly gave way as her belly grew. From time to time, she recalled the sting of her last conversation with Lilianna, who couldn't hide her disappointment. In the brief time that Danusia had been at the academy, Lilianna felt she showed brains and confidence, and she could have had a future a long way away from a mundane life on the farm. Although Lilianna didn't really mean to, she hurt Danusia's feelings, but Danusia had the resilience to get over it for the most part. It certainly helped that she never wanted to be at that academy in the first place.

Lilianna's poor choice of words sprang from her own feelings about children. She had come to terms with not having any of her own, since she and Ihor had tried unsuccessfully for years. Danusia's situation had stirred up some of the old emotions from the deep well that Lilianna thought she had capped for good.

After Danusia left, Lilianna pondered and realized that a gap in her curriculum needed to be filled. She decided to develop revolutionary, far-sighted changes; the young women would now also be taught how to take control of their bodies and know what they were getting into beyond simple romance.

We Do

Within two weeks, Danusia and Mykola were married in a small ceremony at the log-built church that smelled of warm pine, beeswax, and incense. Standing in front of the embroidery-covered altar, the young priest looked down at them as they kneeled together in front of him. He himself would never be married to a woman, and he couldn't help feeling a pang of loss when seeing the obvious love these two people had for each other. He had tried to offer them some pre-marriage counselling but his advice was a little thin. The best he could come up with was to be kind to each other. If he'd known about the baby, he certainly would have had more to say. He was much better at scolding than counselling, except that it was too late anyway.

Mykola's parents set up a small living space for them in the back room of their house and told everyone truthfully that they were happy that Danusia had joined their family. She felt very much at ease in her new home. It was much nicer than Taras' hovel and she didn't have to share the room with Taras' five children.

Mykola fussed around her, ensuring her comfort and warmth. Mykola's parents paid just enough attention to her and fed her well to keep her healthy and strong.

Old Dido was coming to terms with becoming a great-grandfather and spent his evenings hand-carving the head and foot ends of a basinet he was building himself.

Because her own parents were too far away and there was no simple way to communicate with them, Danusia neglected to tell them about her marriage and, later, about the birth of baby Julianna. If she had wanted, she could have sent a dispatch but it would have created a chaos that she couldn't control from a distance.

In any case, she still harboured a stabbing resentment towards them for sending her away without even asking if she wanted to go. Her current life seemed perfect by comparison.

Unannounced

At the end of the school year, Danusia's parents rolled up in a horse cart to bring her home for the summer. They followed the directions to Taras' home, expecting to knock on the door and to be greeted by a surprised and grateful, educated young lady. Instead, Taras delivered the shock of their lives.

There was some shrieking.

There was some arm-waving.

And more oy-yoying.

Finally, after the shockwave subsided and the blame-hurling had exhausted, Danusia's parents loaded back onto the cart and made their way slowly to Stefan's home to find their daughter. Even though they wanted to speed over to it, they needed time to figure out what to do.

They knew that Danusia was still upset with them for sending her away because she hadn't answered any of their letters. This is why they came unannounced, so that she wouldn't have time to run and hide from them. But worse yet, she hadn't informed them of her whole new life that included a husband and a baby, and a completely different path than her parents thought they had set her on.

They both agreed that she had certainly been through a lot and their best approach would be to be as open, kind, and accepting as possible. If they were to get their daughter back, that could be the only approach. If it didn't go well, it would be the end of their relationship; a situation worse than it was already.

Trepidation

Mykola heard a squeaking cart roll up close to his home. He peeked through the split in the cotton curtains of the front window and saw two people he had never met before but who were perfectly blended together in the facial features of his wife. He knew this day was coming, and although the sighting of the parents filled him with dread, he decided to act like a man and greet them outside. He was terrified.

Danusia's parents desperately wanted everything to go well. They had a new son-in-law and, better yet, a new grandchild. They wanted to welcome them to their family, but they were afraid of what could happen in the next few minutes. They were also terrified.

Age Discrimination

Mykola approached the people in the cart, asking politely if they were lost and needed help, pretending not to know who they were right off. He tried to stand tall and he puffed out his chest somewhat. He squinted into the sun that highlighted the soft, blond baby whiskers above his lip.

"Is your daddy home? Or your big brother?" asked Danusia's father, trying very hard to be calm. This young boy could lead him to his daughter and son-in-law. No missteps could be made.

"Oh, why are you looking for them?" asked Mykola, masking the hurt he felt at being spoken to like a child. Danusia's father replied that they had come to see their daughter and Mykola, her new husband.

Danusia's mother spoke up, looking kindly down upon Mykola from her seat on the cart.

"We have had a terrible misunderstanding and we have come to fix it. Where is Danusia?"

Mykola's parents had been in the garden but were alerted by the neighbour's barking dog. They came around the house, saw the cart and the faces of the people, and instantly knew they could be losing the ones they'd grown to love so much. Yes, they too were terrified, of course.

Danusia and the baby had just awoken from a dog-bark-shortened nap. She peeked out the window and was quite taken aback by the scene outside. She quickly gathered up the baby, gave her own hair a finger-combing, and joined ranks with her husband outside, defiantly and steadfastly facing her parents for the first time in months.

"I live here now. With my husband and our daughter," she said, one arm wrapped around the baby, the other arm linking tightly with Mykola.

Hearing about this union was one thing, but actually seeing it, right there in front of them, was yet another shock for Danusia's parents.

Danusia's mother came close to saying it out loud. These two children looked like they were "playing house" with a doll. She dug a thumbnail into her palm, a reminder to say the right things.

But in the moment, she couldn't think of the "right things" and instead, her tears conveyed the message. As she stepped closer to the young couple, at just the right moment, the baby turned her head to look at her grandmother and stretched out her hand towards her.

That was all it took.

The Mending

In the spirit of typical Zustrich hospitality, Mykola's parents hustled everyone inside to sit, eat, and talk things out. The first thing on Danusia's mind was to bring up her banishment to the academy. There was no circling around the subject; she wanted to know why she had been sent away.

As her parents explained and apologized and begged her to understand their motivation, Danusia felt all her anger towards them drain away. Being a mother now herself, she could clearly understand how she too would want the best for her child, even if it meant a difficult sacrifice.

Suddenly a feeling of sadness filled the room, a whiff of impending loss, as a sacrifice was about to be proposed.

Old Dido was sitting at the table, but even before the discussions were completed, he pushed back his chair, made an excuse to leave, and loaded his basinet into the visitor's cart. It was only for a baby after all; it wasn't very heavy.

He, as a wise old man, knew how this scene would end.

Danusia's parents insisted that she and the baby come home with them and let Mykola lead his life unencumbered.

He was still very young and he would find his way without the burden of a wife and child. She could live with them until the baby was older and then she could go back to school if she wanted, but somewhere closer and not expensive because there was a new mouth to feed.

Danusia's mother, in particular, had come around to accepting the situation and was excited at the prospect of having a baby in her home again. She was only thirty-six years old, a very young grandmother. After having come close to losing her daughter forever, she could now have a daughter *and* a granddaughter, sixteen years apart.

Heart to Heart

Mykola had never felt so torn before. He wasn't sure of anything. What would be the right thing to do? He wished he could fly into the future to see how everything would work out. Were Danusia's parents suggesting the best solution? What did his parents think? He needed more time to figure it all out.

He asked if there was any hurry. Could Danusia's parents stay the night so they could all have more time? His parents didn't disagree but wondered where they would put them up to sleep. They didn't want to ask their neighbours for help and they certainly didn't want them to become involved and gossip about the situation.

Danusia's parents agreed that more time was a good idea and they would be perfectly happy to sleep in their cart.

It was a warm, early-summer night, and they had come prepared with makeshift bedding in case they would be delayed along the way. Even when they traveled short distances, they needed to be self-sufficient and self-contained, and they were always prepared with extra supplies in case a wheel broke or a horse went lame.

During and after dinner, the adults debated about what to do, and eventually a plan was agreed upon by all.

All, except Danusia and Mykola.

As the "children", they were not really included in the discussions. It was made clear to them that they should just listen to what the wise elders recommended because only they would know what was best.

Danusia felt it was happening again. No one asked her opinion or desires. She left the room to put the baby down to sleep but to her dismay, she discovered that the basinet was missing. She didn't know what had happened to it and for a minute, until Old Dido explained, she thought she'd been moved out already. Again.

Old Dido apologized for upsetting her. Even though he had jumped to his conclusion too quickly, he still thought he would be right, eventually.

Mykola brought the basinet back into the house and soon the baby was asleep. He took Danusia by the hand and they sought a private place outside to talk. They sat together in a close huddle on a smooth, old log bench carved by Old Dido many years ago. Under the natural arbor of delicate weeping willow branches, a soft, warm breeze slipped over their shoulders.

"Mykola, my heart is absolutely breaking. And even though they are taking charge again and not asking us, I think…I think my parents are right. I should go with them."

"Really? They have almost convinced me too, but I don't want you both to go", said Mykola. His eyes reddened as his lower eyelids filled with tears.

"I feel we're too young for all of this. I don't sleep well; I'm so tired. I really don't know what to do," Danusia sighed heavily, struggling to hold back tears of frustration.

"You know I love you and I want you to do what you think is best," replied Mykola. "Danusia, my parents love you too, but they think we will be moving in different directions soon, as we get older. They said as much."

After some moments of quiet contemplation and tender caresses, they agreed to separate. Mykola would carry on with school and become a "somebody" able to take care of them in the future. In the meantime, Danusia would have the support of her family, and her old familiar surroundings, to make a good life for their child.

In the distance, an owl hooted. Mykola and Danusia laughed softly, hearing it say "Goo good for you… Goo good for you." They were heartened that the mysterious forces of nature agreed with their big decision.

The Dissolution

The new arrangement was struck. Mykola traded the burden of a wife and child, who he could not possibly support himself, for a double broken heart. The rash and impetuous love affair was over and done.

With both sets of parents making sure, the village priest swung an incense-burning censer over the heads of Mykola and Danusia as they knelt together one last time. He had initially objected to conducting any sort of divorce proceeding, but with the delivery of two chickens and a keg of beer, a marriage-dissolution ritual was quickly improvised in return.

Just before Danusia turned to climb into the cart with Julianna, who she had wrapped in a multi-coloured blanket, she pressed her finger to Mykola's sternum and pushed against the bone, saying, "You will feel us here forever."

After they were gone, Mykola tried his best to settle, but he felt that something had happened to his heart. He felt that Danusia had left an imprint on it, about the size and weight of a heavy marble. He learned to live with it, sometimes being able to push the feeling aside, but it was a constant painful reminder of the people he had lost, just as Danusia had pronounced.

His family tried their best to treat him like a normal teenager, as did his friends who were in awe of him for taking such a big, albeit temporary, leap into adulthood. He tried to keep in touch with Danusia and Julianna, hitching rides on transport trucks to see them when he could, but the fire was soon snuffed out by distance and time, and as they made no effort to come to see him, he decided to think of himself as released.

Mykola's Secret

Mykola would think of Danusia and Julianna forever, and he reserved a special place in his heart for them, but he had to let them go so that he could move on. He would never speak of them again, never open the book to that chapter for someone else to read, but he planned the small gesture of sending a birthday card to Julianna every year and, as soon as he was able, he would slip some money into it. No other people would ever need to know.

Devil's People

Two of the inhabitants of Zustrich were old and decaying twin sisters who held self-appointed sway over all other people in the village. They continued to make Mykola's life unbearable. Just as his heart began to heal, the hags gleefully scratched new wounds into it. They would leave their cauldron on a slow boil in their forest cottage to soften the wolf meat in their stew, and come sit on a wooden bench in the Zustrich town square from where they could spy on everyone's movements.

He could hear them cackling while they sat, making sure he heard them criticize his inability to keep a wife and his irresponsibility in caring for his daughter. They laughed at him for thinking he was such a big man, when he was really just a child and should be more concerned with school and the growing fuzz on his face.

The old witches growled, "The whole town knows what you did, Mykola. Be ashamed forever. This is the curse we have put upon you."

They really were the most wicked types, who caused all sorts of havoc for people around them and who eagerly shuffled to church for confession each week to absolve their mighty sins. The priest recognized them from behind the privacy curtain of the confessional with their similar grunts and cracking knee joints as they each crumpled down to kneel on the hard wooden board. They disturbed him with their similar speech patterns, every phrase sounding like an evil incantation. One of them smelled more garlicky than the other, but their sins aligned week after week. As they aged, he urged them to come more often so he could keep their souls cleansed in case they should exit in sudden, timely deaths.

So try as he might, Mykola never felt welcome in his hometown again, and begged his parents to allow him a new start somewhere else. They agreed that this would be the best for all of them, because they too were feeling the hot dragon breath of the old witches. The sooner he was out of sight, the sooner he'd be out of the mean old women's minds, and they could rub their old arthritic hands together and rejoice in focusing on a fresh victim.

Heading Out

It was much harder for Mykola to leave than he expected. First, he had to decide what to take with him, limiting his satchel to a weight he could carry. Then he had to say goodbye to his parents, which was horrible, and leave his familiar surroundings and family home and friends. And if that wasn't hard enough, Mykola had to say goodbye to Old Dido, which was the worst of all because he knew beyond a doubt that Old Dido would be gone by the time Mykola was ever able to return.

Because he had no means of photographing him, Mykola tried to sketch Old Dido's face while he napped in a chair, but the result, with Old Dido's closed eyes and sagging face, made him look dead already. Mykola scrunched up the paper and threw it into the fireplace where it was instantly devoured by hungry orange flames. He could only rely on his memory for Old Dido's facial details, complete with cheek wrinkles, wild grey eyebrows, and the veins that throbbed on both temples.

When it was time to leave the small cottage, Mykola reached to give Old Dido a solid, manly hug, but he lessened his grip after feeling more bones than muscle. This time it was Old Dido who repeated the old village custom by pressing his finger to Mykola's sternum and saying, "You will feel me here forever."

With crystal clarity, it occurred to Mykola that leaving was much worse than staying and enduring the witches' tauntings. He just wasn't old enough to make sense of it all. He should have been able to weather the old ladies, or outlast them at least, but the door had opened for him to explore the whole wide world, or what would be left of it, and there was no staying now. It would be difficult, but he would just have to push his feelings aside and take his adventure to wherever it led him.

Mykola's father suggested hiking along a well-marked trail up and over a hilly region, to arrive at a small town one valley over, just over ten kilometers away. Even though this new town was relatively close as the crow flies, the distance allowed for some differences in dialect and customs to develop. Mykola would learn that those differences could help pinpoint a person's origins with surprising accuracy.

Getting Schooled

Mykola had time to think while he was walking and he decided that if he were to become someone important, he would have to finish high school at least. In his village school, he had shown some talent for writing and for arithmetic, and he was a very good reader from an early age. He was unusual in that he actually enjoyed school because it wasn't difficult for him and, being well-behaved, he suffered none of the punishments meted out to his more careless classmates.

When he arrived in the new town, he asked for directions to the nearest school, which was easy to spot from a distance because of its alternating red and grey brick pattern and its terracotta tile roof. He walked up the stairs and in through the rather daunting wooden front doors, and went straight to the Major School main office. There, an older woman sat filling her fountain pen. Miss Katerina peered at him over her glasses and listened as he explained why he had come.

Well, hmm, this was a new scenario for her! In all her years, Miss Katerina had never seen a boy practically begging to go to school. Could this be some sort of joke?

As Mykola spoke, asking for admission to the school and help in finding some place to live, she realized by his dialect that he had come from her old village, and then she took a guess at why he was in this town today.

"Are the old village witches still alive? Have you run afoul of them?" she asked.

Mykola's ears turned red and hot, and he replied in nearly a whisper, "Yes, they are still alive, and yes, they have turned against me. They cause so much trouble for people. I think God is disappointed in how they turned out and now he's afraid to call them home."

Miss Katerina chuckled in agreement and confided in Mykola, without elaborating, that she had also been one of their victims and she ended up in this town because of them. It was just far enough away that they would never bother following. They behaved in exactly the same strange, evil ways when they were younger. Since she and Mykola had this experience in common, she would see what she could do for him.

Mykola sat down on a hard wooden bench in the office,

waiting for Miss Katerina to come back. She had gone to the Director's office and Mykola wasn't sure how this would turn out. He heard a bell ring and then students talking and laughing as they moved in the hallway between classes. And then it was quiet again. The clock on the wall ticked loudly.

Miss Katerina was gone a long time, it seemed. Mykola was already making plans for his next steps, just in case, when the Director came out of his office and asked him to come see him. He was a stern-looking man with a concealed heart of gold. Miss Katerina had explained the situation and, luckily, there was some extra time available in his busy schedule that day to run a few tests to determine Mykola's grade placement. He assured Mykola that he would be accepted into the school, no matter what the placement tests showed. There was always room for more students.

This was reassuring news and Mykola felt relieved, but he told the Director that he had been in the tenth year and would not settle for going backwards. The Director took no offense, and thought this was a bold boy, striking out on his own. Good for him!

Testing, Testing

The tests were constructed fairly to reveal or confirm an appropriate grade level. Mykola was asked to read aloud from a difficult passage, and although he stumbled on a few unfamiliar words, he was able to get through it quite fluently.

When tested on his comprehension, he answered all the questions correctly. He was asked to deduce and to predict outcomes from events that happened in the passage, and he scored highly in those tasks as well.

Next, he was given a contentious topic and was asked to write a paragraph choosing a position for or against. His content would be evaluated, as well as the clarity of his penmanship. And finally, he was given several mathematical problems that increased in complexity and difficulty. Each problem had a definite answer, and he was asked to show his thought process as he worked his way through.

The Director sat working at his desk and kept one eye on Mykola, watching him concentrate and focus on his work. Not many of the students at this school could show such dedication to proving themselves. When Mykola finished, he was asked to wait on the bench again. After a half hour or so, the Director called in Miss Katerina and they could be heard discussing the results, only in a murmur at best, through the Director's closed door.

Unexpected Result

When the door finally opened, the Director looked serious, perhaps a little cross, as if Mykola had lied about being in tenth year. Then with a broad smile, he announced that Mykola would be entering into the twelfth year class. Mykola was stunned and Miss Katerina felt a smidge of pride for the education Mykola had received in her old hometown, when really it was just his own talents that had shown themselves. The look on Mykola's face changed suddenly from happiness to worry since he didn't have anywhere to live or any means to survive. Miss Katerina suggested that he could stay with her in the little cabin on her property. If Mykola would help with chores, she would count that as his payment towards room and board. Mykola was having a great day. He thanked Miss Katerina for her consideration and then looked to the Director for approval of the plan. With a nod of his head, the Director sent Mykola off to explore his new surroundings.

Lodged

Miss Katerina's humble abode sat at the top of a hill about half a kilometer from the school. In the morning, it was easy to get to the school building on the downhill run, but returning at the end of the day, uphill, with books in his satchel, caused Mykola to breathe heavily. Over time, his legs and lungs got used to the rise in elevation and soon he had no problems at all. During those months, he was also growing in height and muscle and changing into a handsome, young man.

Because he was unable to return to his home, for now at least, the only way that Mykola could communicate with his parents was by sending a message with a dispatcher. He tried to send a note once a week so they would know that he was studying and doing well, so they would know he was safe and cared for, and that he thought of them every day. His parents, in turn, sent notes back with updates of their own, words of encouragement, and messages of love.

At the end of the school year, Mykola graduated at the top of his class in mathematics and near the top in all other subjects. He had made a few new friends and he had forged a good friendship with Miss Katerina. When his classes were finished and he had no homework to keep him busy in the evenings, a roiling feeling began to grow in his stomach. As he talked about it with Miss Katerina over dinner one night, she helped him recognize what was bothering him. He was simply homesick.

The Director encouraged Mykola to become a teacher someday to impart his knowledge to the next generation. Mykola agreed that it would be a fine thing to do, but he hadn't made up his mind yet regarding his future. He wasn't sure where he would be, but he was fairly certain that he wouldn't be in this town for very long. Without being able to return to his hometown and having reached the end of his schooling, he was looking forward to moving on.

For the moment, though, it seemed practical to follow the Director's advice. With a strong recommendation letter in his hand, he met with the Director of the Minor school, a few blocks away from the Major school from which he had just graduated. This Director was quite impressed and promised Mykola a position of teacher's assistant in the fall after the summer break. In the meantime, he would have to find work to tide him over the next two months.

Mykola thanked the Director and walked back out onto the street, wondering what to do next. As he wandered back towards Miss Katerina's, he saw the small community gathering-place in the distance. He'd been there once or twice before, and he knew there was a posting board that he could check out.

Sure enough, this town had plenty of work for strong, young men. Most of the town's population was either too old or too young for anything requiring physical strength, so if someone was available to haul, shovel, build, or move, they could be employed in no time.

Working with Horses

A farmer nearby, who had just lost his son in an accident, desperately needed extra help. Mykola was given a job in the horse stables, mucking out the stalls, feeding and brushing the horses, and driving the horse cart to move supplies. He was even allowed to ride a horse occasionally. The large ones frightened him so he preferred to ride the big pony who was small enough for Mykola to nearly touch the ground with his toes, but large enough to carry Mykola's weight comfortably. The pony never bucked and he walked slowly, so it wasn't really like riding a horse at all.

Mykola learned to harness the horses to the cart, and when the farmer was out of sight, Mykola would encourage them to a lively dash, which they seemed to enjoy as much as Mykola himself. He never pushed them too hard because he didn't want to tip over the cart. Being careful was a good way to stay employed, and alive.

The summer moved slowly, with hot days settling in for a long stretch. The farmhands rose with the dawn and tried to get as much work done as they could before the noonday sun reached its peak. A short nap under a tree after lunch always helped to refresh their strength. Later in the evening they would get together when it was cooler, to eat and drink and relax after a hard day's work, and soon they were yawning and going off to bed to start the daily cycle over again. Mykola was usually the first one to leave because he still had to get home to Miss Katerina's cabin. He wasn't sure how much longer she'd allow him to stay because he wasn't able to do his chores there any more, so he proposed a weekly payment from his wages and she agreed to it. She actually valued his company more than his money, but the money didn't hurt.

The horses seemed to know Mykola. They raised their heads and turned their ears in the direction of his approach. Mykola talked to them kindly and allowed them the thrill of a good run. He made sure that they had whatever they needed to get through their days. The horses repaid Mykola by never pinning him against their stalls and never flinging snot onto his shirt, as they had for other keepers. They tried hard to listen to his commands when attached to the cart, where they cooperated as a smooth-pulling team.

The other animals on the farm also responded favourably to Mykola. The cows seemed to enjoy the peaceful atmosphere and their milk flowed easily. Mykola could read their moods through the tone of their mooing and the way they met his gaze with their big, brown eyes. The pigs, however, showed a little obstinance from time to time, not wanting to heave their heavy bodies out from their comfortable but stinking pigsties. Mykola had to persist to get them going. He sympathized with them because they were smart and no doubt aware that, regularly around Easter, one of them disappeared no matter how they behaved.

As the summer season was ending, the farmer remarked to Mykola that he was very pleased with the way things worked out. The animals responded to Mykola, the farm was running well, and even though he didn't expect a young man with Mykola's promise to stay forever, he asked him if he would agree to stay a little longer. He missed his own son greatly and Mykola's presence helped to ease his sadness and his unending workload. They would be heading into the fall harvest time soon.

Bored Witches

The old wicked twins sat on their bench, feeling very bored. Most of the people that they took great pleasure in attacking had either moved away or died. Such was the backfiring result of their nastiness. They began to think about what else they could do to amuse themselves. They made a short list of anyone still alive and present who might have slighted them in any way in the past. At the top of the list was Old Dido.

Old Dido's cottage was in the forest on the opposite side of the village from the old hags' home. He had purposely chosen that location to live as far away from them as possible. When he and they were much younger, in the same village, going to the same school, there was a rumour going around that the evil twin girls had taken a liking to him.

They began to appear next to him any time he was alone; as he walked to school, or as he sat in a quiet spot for lunch, or when he was looking for books on the long, high shelves of the library. They seemed to appear out of nowhere, and when they saw him, they would chant in unison something about Cupid and love. This absolutely made his skin crawl and he tried to stay away from them, but they kept finding him. It was hard to defend himself with two against one.

Then for his fifteenth birthday, young Old Dido planned to throw himself a bonfire party and he invited all his friends. The twins found out about it, and they were not happy, at all, at being excluded. When they confronted him, he panicked, and for lack of better judgement and foresight, gave them a false location for the party just to shake them off. But, of course, when they arrived there later that evening, they realized they had been duped, and because they were at least half-human, their feelings were sorely bruised. At the time, the young witches hadn't yet realized or fully developed their cursing powers. This is why young Old Dido escaped unharmed.

Until now.

Old Dido rarely had unexpected guests at his cottage, but whenever there was a knock on the door, he was excited at the prospect of a visit. At times, it would be a hunter who had injured himself instead of his prey, at times it was Mykola, oh and sometimes it was the fair, old maiden seeking some special company.

On this day, when he enthusiastically opened the door, he came face-to-face with his worst nightmare.

They had come.

After all those years.

They had come for him.

A Drink?

Old Dido felt the hairs stand up on the back of his neck and his knees became instantly weak. He tried not to look too petrified in front of the witches because he knew they could smell fear, but they had sure caught him by surprise. After a moment, the feeling began to return to his legs, and he demanded abruptly, "What do you two want?"

The old, decrepit, pinch-faced women declared sweetly, "Nothing. We both are simply bored. We picked some lovely mushrooms in the forest this morning and we've come to share some with you because we haven't seen you in a long, long time."

Before Old Dido could shut and lock the door, they pushed their way into his home and, setting a basket on his table, they began to pull out some mushrooms to leave behind for him. Old Dido knew more about the varieties than they suspected but he played dumb, even complimenting them on their selections. He knew, of course, that some of them were highly poisonous. He could tell by the little white ridge around the edge of the cap that differentiated the safe from the deadly.

He thanked them for the unexpected gift and asked if they would like to share a drink of his specially distilled 'shine. He reached way up to the top shelf of his cabinet where his "special drink for special visits" was safely stored.

Bringing the pewter pitcher and three of his best crystal glasses to the table, he poured the clear liquid and gently pushed two of the glasses towards the women. In sync, they greedily grabbed and drained the drinks in two large, noisy gulps. Old Dido copied them right afterwards, exhaling with a loud "Ahhhh", and releasing a generous belch. Not to be out-done, the two women waited just a few seconds and then let out their own loud belches, double in volume. Old Dido laughed and congratulated them on a burp well done! They took the compliment and tried again, but sadly found they had run out of gas.

The hags got up to leave and suggested vociferously that Old Dido should make himself a hearty mushroom soup for supper. It would fill him up and make him feel so good.

He nodded and promised that he would do just that, and bade them a good evening and a safe walk home. As they shuffled out of his cottage, disappearing into the darkness on the trail back to the village, Old Dido threw away their two glasses. Their nasty lips had touched them and spoiled them forever. Then he refilled the safe drink compartment and the poison drink compartment, differentiated by a hidden switch in the handle. It would only be a matter of time before the witches would regret coming to his home at all.

Church Bells

The church in Mykola's home village had three bells in its tower, tuned to three different pitches. The smallest and fastest bell with the highest pitch was reserved for happy occasions, such as marriages, christenings, and other celebrations. The second, a medium-sized bell with a medium pitch was used for regular church services on Sundays and for other masses during the week. The third bell was the largest, heaviest, slowest bell with the lowest pitch. It tolled only for funerals.

As Mykola's parents were returning from the market, they heard three bells ringing in succession for six seconds each. The heaviest rang for six seconds to call everyone to the old witch's funeral. The heaviest rang again for another six seconds to call everyone for her twin. The third, the smallest, fastest, highest pitched bell, rang for six seconds to signal the joyous occasion. And the pattern repeated over and over again.

In his excitement, the bellringer got a little carried away. When he heard that not just one, but both devious, old, awful women had died by accidental mushroom juice overdose, he started ringing the bells well in advance of the funeral that would take place that day, the same day that they were found. No one, least of all the priest, wanted their bodies above ground for any longer than absolutely necessary.

The bellringer had done double-tolling before, when more than one person was being ushered to the other-world, but this time he added his own giddy flourish with the Celebration bell. It took very little time for the villagers to understand the code. They all dropped what they were doing and rushed to the church to see if their guess was correct, and when they saw the old women, dehydrated and feeble, lying in their rough-hewn caskets, there were hoots and hollers of joy, which under any other circumstance would have been considered terribly inappropriate.

Safe to Go Home

Just before her lunchtime break, Miss Katerina received an unexpected message from an old friend who announced the witches' death. Upon reading the note, she felt absolutely delighted and relieved to hear the news. She could barely contain herself, her happiness radiating like tingles and rainbows. Even the Director noticed. Those witches had made her life miserable and even though they had claimed to be immortal, they clearly, thankfully, were not.

The news, however, brought her as much dread as joy. She didn't look forward to sharing the news with Mykola because she knew full well what would happen next. For a moment, she considered not telling him at all.

Later as she chopped vegetables by her kitchen window, Miss Katerina observed Mykola as he returned from the farm and loped up the path to the cabin where he'd lived for almost two years. Normally he looked tired at the end of the day and in need of a hearty meal. But today he seemed to have an extra spring in his step. Just a coincidence?

Her happiness had completely worn off by then, in the face of the realization that the end of the witches meant the end of her relationship with Mykola. This could be the last time he'd be coming "home". The last time he would come for dinner. The last time he might make her smile. The only obstacles to Mykola's return had just been removed and he was going to leave her today. She just knew it.

Indeed, he was already packing his satchel when Miss Katerina knocked on his door. When he opened it, she stepped inside and saw what he was doing.

"You already know?" she asked.

"About the funeral? Yes, I received a message this morning. The dispatcher found me at the farm."

"Are you...are you leaving tonight?" she asked, hoping he would say no.

"Absolutely! This is what I've been waiting for. I can go home now and everything will be back to normal again."

Miss Katerina was floating in a sea of emotions. This young man had unwittingly stolen a piece of her heart and she missed him terribly already.

"I understand you have to leave, and in many ways I am very happy for you. I'm sorry, I didn't expect to be quite so emotional, but you have become a good friend and I simply feel so sad at this very moment."

Mykola stopped what he was doing and searched her face. He didn't expect this reaction from her because it was always understood that he would leave as soon as the path was cleared. She picked up one of his shirts and folded it tenderly, a tear escaping down her cheek, betraying her resolve.

"Oh, I don't have to leave right away. Hmm, yes, it will be too dark to walk in the forest soon. Let's have a nice dinner and I'll leave tomorrow morning instead," Mykola offered.

"That sounds like a good idea," she replied, trying hard to smile.

Miss Katerina had obviously become attached to Mykola and she worried that she would be lonely again. On the other hand, offering her cabin to Mykola, who had been a complete stranger at the time, had worked out very well for her. So there was no reason why she couldn't find someone else to fill his spot in the future. A bright side peeked over the dark edge.

Over dinner, Mykola thanked Miss Katerina sincerely for everything she had done for him. She told him how, besides being a good friend, he was also a welcome diversion from her years of living a rather solitary life. His cheerful face reminded her to be happy. He had been an outstanding student who made the whole school proud, and while he worked for the farmer, his dedication to the task and his connection with the animals was well-known around the town. She knew he would be successful wherever he ended up. She also knew that this day was coming.

They talked long into the night, recounting their first meeting at the school, some of the funny things that happened since then, and their hopes and plans for the future. By the time they went to bed, Miss Katerina felt more at ease and accepting of the situation. And oblivious Mykola finally understood what had been going on.

The next morning, she left for work before he'd awoken. She didn't want to see him leaving for good. No long goodbyes.

The day was clear and warming up. Mykola felt his excitement grow and now he was in a big hurry to get home. Running downhill, with his satchel hung over his shoulders like a large rucksack, he almost lost his footing and windmilled his arms wildly, trying to catch his balance.

He startled a team of horses pulling a cart, causing the driver to shout out a warning meant for both Mykola and the horses. The cart's driver just happened to be Mykola's employer, the farmer.

"Hey, you're late for work! What are you doing?" shouted the farmer.

Mykola shouted back to him that he had to leave on short notice.

"I'm sorry, but I can go home now! I appreciate all you've done for me. Goodbye!"

He took off running, leaving the farmer a little angry for being abandoned without warning, and a little jealous that he couldn't just take off like that himself. He longed for his carefree days before responsibilities weighed him down more each year.

As he passed the school, Mykola noticed the Director at the front doors welcoming students inside. He stopped for a moment, caught his breath, and thanked the Director for his kindness and support. He explained excitedly that he was heading back home again.

"Oh yes, I heard about those old women. Miss Katerina looked very happy yesterday, but today she looks a little down. She's going to miss you," said the Director, who had expected to see Mykola flying by at any minute.

Miss Katerina could hear their brief conversation from the short distance to the door, but having already said her goodbyes, she chose to stay inside.

Mykola's Return

There is never any happier person than a mother whose child has returned from being away. Mykola's father, Stefan, was happy too, but his mother felt it in a different, deeper way. When they caught sight of him, oy-yoy, coming out of the trees at the far edge of the field, they both dropped their garden tools and rushed into the house to throw a meal together and to fluff up his bed.

Stefan fetched Old Dido in the horse cart and brought him to the house. Old Dido was grateful for the change of scenery and was looking forward to being doted upon, but he didn't expect to hear the great news that Mykola was already waiting for him.

After dinner they all sat in front of the fireplace and talked about the future. Mykola's parents tried not to stare but were continually drawn to looking at their son who had changed so much in the time he had been away. He had grown and gotten stronger, and smarter, and more independent. They both knew that this village was too small for him and that he really should move on to some place even bigger than the town one valley away.

But Mykola resisted. He had just come back and wanted some time to enjoy his life here as he had before the witches precipitated his exile. Although it had worked out well for him while he was away, it made him realize that he'd taken a lot for granted back home. Now he was ready to contribute more and to help his family as they had helped him.

War Rumblings

The Big War had started but was being waged far away so they were largely unaffected. Whenever Stefan had a chance to borrow a newspaper from someone, he read of invasions and troop movements to the east, and he worried that the war could move in closer to them. Certainly it was only a matter of time before their peaceful existence would be turned upside down.

For the time being, Mykola's parents had resolved to stay put, since it would be difficult to uproot themselves and Old Dido, but they didn't want their son to risk conscription into the army. There were rumours of too few volunteers and that soon the officials would swing through villages and gather up the young to fight.

Rain Dropping

A few weeks passed and the weather turned foul. Sheets of cold rain fell from the sky for days, puddles formed everywhere, and Old Dido's cottage roof was leaking in several places. The old man hadn't felt well for several days, coughing and wheezing, and his thoughts were more muddled lately. He was convinced that he would have the strength to fix the thatched roof himself. A deep, rumbly cough shook him as he struggled to put a ladder up to the eave by the front door, and he clambered up slowly, trying to reach the thatching. He hadn't dressed appropriately for the conditions and the rain was soaking what little hair was left on his head, running into his eyes and down his neck inside the collar of his thin jacket. It was bitterly cold and getting windy. With some resignation, he just gave up. He would set out some pots to catch the water and learn to live with the uneven rhythm of the falling droplets.

Later that evening, Old Dido felt hot and clammy with fever. He was shivering under four wool blankets. Unable to get himself something to eat, he felt weak and was finding it increasingly hard to breathe. A few hours later, he was sleeping on and off, hallucinating or dreaming, trying to catch his breath. He hallucinated a halo-like aura around Mykola when he came to check on him. He could see it as clearly as if it were real.

Mykola stayed with him through the night, listening to the old man's wheezing, trying to cool him down with a cold cloth to his forehead. Because of Old Dido's age and poor physical condition, it didn't take very long. Before Mykola had a chance to fetch his parents, Old Dido whispered his final words into Mykola's ear, pressing out the scant breath that he managed to take in. He used his final seconds to eke out the words that Mykola would never divulge.

"Discard…the poison…pewter. …I…did it…for you."

By the next afternoon, the heavy bell began tolling for six seconds, over and over. No one hooted or hollered, no one ran. Old Dido's somber procession, led by Mykola, made its way from the church to the graveyard with perfect respect and grace.

A Village Away

Life without Old Dido felt so strange; Mykola had counted on his counsel many times in his life. He continued to talk out loud to him, pretending he was just sitting, listening, silently mulling in his chair. By the time Mykola had talked things out, it was as if Old Dido had helped him once again.

Just before dawn, Mykola was roused from his bed. He wouldn't have time to discuss anything with Old Dido's spirit. All three bells in the tower were ringing simultaneously, in a panicky pattern of no pattern at all. Some years ago, it had been established by village council that this would be the signal for imminent danger. The conscription enforcers were on their way.

Mykola's parents urged him to leave again, right away, to stay safe and alive. They'd all talked about what they would do when the time came, they'd had some practise saying goodbye last time he left, and his parents only wanted what was best for him. They would stay and manage, or they would hide out in Old Dido's cottage if need be, but they weren't willing to leave. It was a stubborn position and made no sense to stay in the line of danger, but it was their decision nevertheless.

Mykola's father supplied him with a rough map of roadways and landmarks that would lead him to a town some fifty kilometers away, a town bigger than Miss Katerina's that prospered from mining in the nearby mountain range, from sawmills that processed lumber from logs that were floated down the wide river, and from the rich black soil that yielded bushels of fresh produce every year. The location of the town would put Mykola much closer to a big seaport, a sure way to escape if worst came to worst.

On the map was an address of a man named Lubomir who met Mykola's father many years ago when they worked together on a farm. Lubomir and Stefan hadn't kept in touch and Stefan wasn't certain whether Lubomir still lived there, but Mykola would find out, hopefully soon enough.

As Mykola walked down the side of the dirt roads to get to his destination, he had to pay attention and take action if he heard a convoy of army trucks approaching from ahead or behind. Even though the battlegrounds were far away, the trucks loaded with soldiers, munitions, and supplies cut through the peaceful land to get to the front.

Several times, Mykola leapt into a nearby high-grassed ditch or hid breathing heavily behind a dense stand of trees so as not to be seen by the soldiers flying by in their final few hours left on Earth. The trucks left a trail of thick dust, and gravel pellets shot out from under their deep-treaded tires. Mykola could hear the boys singing loudly, songs of valour and bravery meant to ease the journey and bolster their purpose. He felt sorry for them for being tricked into someone else's conflict and he was determined to avoid it.

It took him several days to walk the distance at a leisurely pace. Along the way, he stopped for food in small villages, buying fruits and bread from roadside vendors or small shops. With his friendly demeanor and honest face, he found people willing to put him up for the night and only once had a nasty encounter, finding a man hovering and murmuring near his sleeping spot.

His father's directions were excellent, given the time that had passed since the last time he travelled that way himself. Mykola found a signpost at the edge of a road, its location matching with the X marked on the map, and Lubomir's name was hand-carved into it.

The farm had a large barn and acres of planted wheat, a small herd of cattle, and several pigs and chickens. As Mykola headed up the long cart path to the house, he wondered what would be in store for him and whether he would find a place of temporary refuge.

A man was picking through a toolbox, looking for a screwdriver to tighten the bucket-lowering crank for the deep fresh water well. Hearing Mykola crunch the cart path pebbles under his boots, the man looked up and took notice of the stranger approaching.

Before Mykola had even started to introduce himself, Lubomir stuck out his left hand and gave Mykola an awkward backward-feeling handshake, eyeing him up and down as if scoping out his strength. He laughed and said, "You don't have to tell me who you are, son of Stefan. You look a lot like him."

Handing over a note, Mykola stood back while Lubomir read it, nodding his head in comprehension. He had a number of farm boys here and all of them were worried about the conscription, but there had been no hint of imminent threat in the area. Lubomir told Mykola that, of course, he was welcome to stay if he joined the work crew to help out. But in fact, he would have sheltered Mykola even if there hadn't been any work to do. In the note, Stefan reminded him, "I once saved you. Now please save my son."

"Your timing is perfect. The harvest is about to begin." And then Lubomir added, "We can always use an extra hand around here."

The Grand Barn

Towards the end of October, the weather had cooled down considerably and the landscape began to change as the trees, gardens, and grasses began to shut down for their winter rest. Farmers, sons, and farmhands worked hard on all the acres and orchards in the area to bring in the harvest before the first frost, and grandmothers, wives, and daughters worked at preserving food to get them through the winter.

By the time it was all done, everyone was ready for the big celebration in the Grand Barn, named for its enormous size, not its beauty. It was the annual gathering on Lubomir's property for food and music and dance, and for the splendid moonshine that had been fermented to well-practised perfection.

Olena gazed up at the old rafters and breathed in the smell of hay, old tools, and weathered wood. In spite of it being old, with a few wall planks missing, and its spider webs, and its cooing barn doves that made a mess, she loved the Grand Barn, with its enormous doors that, when opened wide, seemed to let the whole world in.

She had fond childhood memories of herself and her friends sneaking into the barn regularly to play and hide from each other. At one end, someone had put up a swing with thick boat ropes attached to the roof beam high, high above their heads. The swing's seat was a plank of wood about three feet wide and could easily hold children three across, more if standing and holding on for dear life. The more children, the more powerfully it would swing from one impossibly far end to the other, and with a well-timed jump, they would fly into a soft pile of hay.

The barn filled up quickly with people young, old, and in between, eager to have some fun after days of backbreaking work. Laughter, voices, and music raised the noise level and reverberated richly off the walls and high ceiling of the barn. The talented musicians played their instruments with great enthusiasm and encouraged everyone to dance.

Ivan switched back and forth between fiddle and banjo, his wife Olya looking on with admiration and pride. His thick carpenter's fingers moved deftly on the necks of the instruments, impossibly precisely.

Thomas on accordion, Nevena on dulcimer, and Slawko and Sonia on flutes all added to the revelry and energy in the room. Shy Roman unleashed himself with drumstick torrents on homemade drums. This was the town band, expected at each occasion, and counted on for raising the mood of the crowd to forget their aches and pains, and to just have a good time.

On a Dare

It was clear that someone in a group of young men had come up with a great idea, a great dare, a great show-off opportunity, and posed a challenge to the others who seized upon it and rushed over to the swing. They marked the first jump and bellowed with appreciation. They each took turns standing on the plank, swinging higher and faster.

Attracted by the boisterous shouting, many of the people in the barn turned to gather around to watch the competition and some side-bets were made. Soon everyone had a stake in the results. This only emboldened the young men who took turns to fly farther than the one before them. Landing short meant immediate disqualification, and short-lasting teasing and shame.

Olena held on to a thick post for balance while she stood on an old barrel to get a better view of the crazy ones who were trying so hard to win. As the competition continued, and when only three young men were left, they begged the crowd to move back to give them more space.

Now Olena could see the men when they were swinging and how they behaved when they waited for their turn. There was a new one among them, one slightly taller and a little older than the rest. His hair was light brown, sun-bleached from working the fields, and his shoulders and arms were strong from baling hay. He certainly had a confidence without arrogance, as he encouraged the others for a fair fight while clearly winning up to this point. With his extra height and weight, he had no problem jumping further than the rest, but instead of the others complaining about his physical advantage, they acknowledged Mykola's achievement with hearty slaps on the back and calls to compete again next year.

As they all split up and mingled back into the crowd, Olena jumped off the barrel and headed over to where the winner stood drinking a well-deserved flask of 'shine. She wanted to get his attention, but she was sure he wouldn't be interested in someone her age. She guessed he was at least four, perhaps five years older? Maybe he was with someone already, but she would make an effort to be noticed in any case. She flounced by him, glancing over her shoulder, congratulating him on his win. He looked up but seemed to barely acknowledge her. In truth, he was rather taken by her graceful beauty and blue, blue eyes, but because she appeared young, he kept his feelings to himself.

He had spied her standing on the barrel watching the competition. She didn't even know that his win was for, and because of, her.

Chapter 3

In the New Country 1948–1967

Settling In

Immigrants from war-torn Europe arrived in Montreal in droves, travelling by train from Pier 21 in Halifax, and settling wherever someone would take them in. Olena, in her early twenties, and her husband Mykola, four years older, along with their two young sons Marko and Peter, were greeted by first-cousin-somehow-removed Helena and her husband Gregory who had sponsored them at the last minute, just before they would have otherwise emigrated to Argentina.

Although the family connection with Helena and Gregory was a bit tenuous, Olena and Mykola were eternally grateful, and in the absence of closer relations, they forged a tight bond with them. Helena and Gregory had prepared their second-floor attic space for the extra people, having already allocated their better-insulated back bedroom to a professor who had arrived earlier and who was willing to pay good money. Helena and Gregory's only son, Robert, had moved away from Montreal to Hamilton two years before Mykola and Olena arrived. It was Robert's bedroom that became an income-generating space for his parents. The attic would become a bonus for them.

Olena and Mykola were happy to be safe and alive, and able to get their lives restarted on foreign soil. They had languished in limbo in a Displaced Persons camp for nearly four years, living in rough-hewn barracks with little privacy and no hope of returning home. But under those tough circumstances, good things happened too. Their children were born there, closely one after the other, and were healthy and cute. Olena and Mykola made strong-bonded friendships, the special kind that can only happen when sharing adverse experiences.

They had sailed across the roiling Atlantic in November, a risky, rough passage on the *Nea Hellas,* a Greek-owned ocean liner ill-equipped to detect underwater mines. Shouting into a bullhorn over crashing waves, the Captain of the ship assured them that all would be fine, but his worried expression conveyed other possibilities.

Standing in line at Immigration along with many of their camp friends who also chose Canada as their haven, Olena was relieved to feel her seasickness already start to fade away. That meant it wasn't pregnancy-related nausea, only a temporary inconvenience. She'd had enough of childbirth and couldn't bear to have more children, especially now when they were heading into an uncertain time.

The unilingual immigration officer was concerned about Olena and Mykola's language skills, but having learned several languages as students in school, they had more confidence than he did. Mykola, in particular, had a natural ability to mimic localized accents and switched them up for comic effect when telling a story.

Eventually they attended English language workshops as time permitted, but they also learned to read, write, and speak English from local newspapers, radio, and from their children who picked up proper English with lightning speed at school and a good mix of rude English and French by playing with kids on the street.

Not long after arriving, Mykola found a decent job nearby, and later with Marko and Peter established in a new school and new routines, Olena was freed up to find herself a job. They would try to live on one salary and stash the rest into their "promising a future" jar. Their one early extravagance was a telephone of their own, which Olena thought would help them learn English.

She used the phone to call Mykola at work if he was late, and she used it to call Helena who lived right below them. Gregory was usually the one who answered and Olena could hear him shout, "Helena, Olena's calling!"

A Service to Society

Olena invented what she called "her little social service". From her big, thick phonebook, she chose random numbers from the White Page listings and dialed them, waiting for someone to answer who might engage in a little English conversation. She would always count up to fifteen rings before hanging up to give the person time to get to the phone from outside or from the bathroom.

Most times, people just hung up, but every once in a while, she would hit upon someone who wanted to chat. The chatters were typically people who were lonely or bored, and who appreciated the contact to brighten their day.

Unbeknownst to Olena though, more than once, these little random acts actually brought people back from the brink, when their loneliness had put them in a dark, isolated place.

Olena's calling literally brought someone in from the ledge, the distraught man finding it impossible to ignore a ringing phone. It always sounded louder to him than to normal people, its jarring tone slicing into any delusions he was having. On that day, Olena's persistent ringing made it impossible for him to carry out his suicidal mission. He leaned back with a sigh and laid his palms flat against the bricks, feeling his way sideways across the ledge back to the window, falling head-long back into his drab, empty room.

Grabbing the receiver at ring number fourteen, he caught it just in time to answer before Olena gave up on him. Just in time to not give up on himself.

Need More Space

Olena and Mykola's goal was to get out from under Gregory and Helena's roof as soon as possible and find a place they could buy and pay off a little each month. Mykola was working at a corner Dépanneur, serving customers from behind the counter. He was good with money and could figure out exact change without using a pencil. His boss liked that he was fast and friendly, and that he could pump through a lot of customers throughout the day.

Sometimes to give him a break, his boss would send him out on deliveries in the neighbourhood, and that's how Mykola came to find out about an apartment for sale in a stacked triplex nearby, with an iconic Montreal black and grey, steep and narrow staircase that twisted at the top.

Research

Olena had the early shift at a textile factory, which meant getting up at five-thirty in the morning to catch a long bus ride across town. By the time she arrived back home again in late afternoon, it had been a long day and she was exhausted. It was summer and the days were hotter than she liked. On the way home, the bus was always crowded with workers who'd been sweating all day, with garlic and spices leaching from their pores. She was tired of standing next to people who had no regard for personal space and who were nose-blind to their own exposed armpits as they held on to overhead bars and straps.

In the small bathroom retrofitted under the sloping gable roof, she splashed her face with some cold water and drank a cup as well, instantly feeling some energy return to her limbs. But her day wasn't over yet. The children would be coming home from school and supper must be made and then cleaned up, and if she gave herself a moment's rest, it would be a moment less to get things done. She was not in the mood for anything out of the ordinary.

Mykola's instincts regarding Olena were pretty accurate by now, honed through trial and error. He'd learned not to spring new ideas onto her because they'd be met with outright rejection. He'd learned to research his new proposals thoroughly so that he'd be ready to defend his position and satisfy any concerns. And he'd learned not to interrupt Olena's rare naps because sleep was precious to her and she'd rip out his left eye if he woke her up.

When he found out about the apartment for sale, he sought out advice from anyone who came to the store: his boss and co-workers, a lawyer who shopped there, and other apartment owners in the area. Anyone who came to the store who looked well-off enough to own property was asked, and the same three pieces of advice, for good or for bad, were repeated often.

"Find an old lady whose husband has died, who is selling to move in with her children."

"Buy straight from her without a real estate agent. You can get a better price because she won't have to pay commission."

"Speak to her directly and honestly, and convince her that you will be the best next owners. People want to know their home will be in good hands."

Mykola did the math to figure out monthly payments and he asked the banker, who came to buy milk and candy for his mistress every second day, for help in securing the loan. He had his whole plan worked out and now it was time to broach the subject with Olena.

On a nice day, he would take Olena and the boys to Mount Royal for a picnic and to play in the park. There he would lightly mention something he'd been thinking about, an idea that was just an idea but, you know, what do you think?

He would soft-pedal it like it didn't really matter, like there was no urgency, like there was no commitment whatsoever.

The Proposal

On a fresh and breezy Saturday, under a big blue sky that symbolized endless possibilities to him, he started his dance. First, a toe in the water.

"Olena, do you like where we're living now?"

She replied that it wasn't ideal. They needed more room for the growing boys and they needed to get away from the loving but sometimes prying eyes of Helena and Gregory. She asked him what he thought and he replied that he agreed.

So far, so safe.

After a few quiet minutes, letting the thought soak in, Mykola waded deeper and said he thought it was time for them to move to a place of their own. It couldn't be grand and it couldn't be new, but it could be more private and it could have more than two rooms.

Unbeknownst to Mykola, Olena had already heard about the old lady's pending sale and was eager but apprehensive about bringing up the subject. They had saved a bit of money but thinking of buying a place was a big deal and she didn't want to pressure Mykola. And he didn't want to pressure her. Their match was also made in heaven, without the mushrooms.

Mykola ventured slowly into giving some details. He'd heard of an apartment being sold by an old woman, he'd asked people for advice, he'd done the math on how much it would cost, and as he spoke, carefully and calmly, he kept expecting the push-back he'd experienced before when important stressful topics needed to be discussed. Olena listened patiently, having already decided that she was all-in.

Owning a place was possible and they needed to get started. Everyone had mortgages and they were not dying from them. They each had jobs and were mostly, not always, successful at squirreling away her paycheque every week. In a few years, the boys would be able to deliver newspapers or shovel snow to become a little more financially independent.

Mykola paused to watch his children run, kicking a ball with other boys they had just met. The park was busy with people speaking different languages and enjoying the perfect weather. He sensed that his tactic was going well, so he continued to reveal more of the details that he'd considered.

Olena went along with this, trying to look a little resistant, as she knew that would be expected, but she mostly just let it flow because it was going in a direction that was good for all of them. She loved Mykola for being so rational and careful. Some of her friends' husbands were idiots, rashly making bad decisions and leaving big messes behind. But not Mykola. He'd done the legwork. His pitch was solid. All that was left was to approach the lady and get the deal done.

The Approach

The doorbell rang. It was a sunny Sunday afternoon and Isabella had returned from attending mass at her church. She wiped her hands on a dishrag in the kitchen where she had started to knead some dough for bread. Ah well, she would confess next week for having worked on a Sunday.

Opening the inner door to the small vestibule that was designed to keep the cold or the heat out of the apartment, she peered through the window of the outer door to see who it was. Two people who looked familiar, maybe she had seen them in the neighbourhood before? They were probably collecting money for one charity or another, or trying to convert her to some other religion. Huh, fat chance!

Olena and Mykola had put on their best clothes, to look like they were clean, responsible, respectable people, which they were. They said they had heard that she was selling her apartment and they asked if they could come in to discuss the sale with her. Isabella was a cautious woman and didn't like to be outnumbered so she made the excuse of not being able to neglect her bread at the moment or it wouldn't rise properly.

"Please come back tomorrow," she said, "and we can talk over a good, thick slice with Praszek's butter from down the street."

The next day when Olena and Mykola returned, Isabella opened the door wide and invited them in. On the table, the promised bread and butter was laid out on a platter, a sure sign of welcome. And at the table sat Isabella's son, Antonio, who lived with her and had been out of high school for a year. Antonio didn't say a word. He only nodded his head towards the strangers and then stole glances at Olena when Mykola wouldn't notice. She had long, brown, flowing hair, and her blue, blue eyes pierced Antonio's heart. He couldn't help falling in love on the spot.

An Offer

With everyone seated at the dining room table, Mykola took the lead on making the proposal. He said they had heard that her home was for sale and they would like to buy it. It looked like a fine home, it was in a good area, and it would be a good place for their family. It was small enough so they had already seen enough of it to be certain, and it would be easy to keep clean. Would she consider them suitable to take over from her? Would she consider a private sale without realtor interference, and perhaps a drop in price? How soon could they move in?

Isabella knew exactly why they had come. Her lawyer, who was also her cousin and a frequent shopper at Mykola's store, had tipped her off the night before. She cut thick slices of bread and slowly smeared a good amount of soft, yellow butter on them, making Olena and Mykola wait for her response. Even Antonio couldn't take it any more.

"Ma! Say something!" he shouted.

And that's when she dropped the bomb.

She wasn't selling just her apartment. She owned all three in the triplex. If someone was to buy, they had to buy all three.

Mykola's head jerked back at the same time as his eyebrows shot straight up. Olena's eyes widened as she tried to stay cool in the aftershock. What had started out as a fairly straightforward proposition suddenly became a lot more complicated and seemingly out of reach. But Isabella wasn't finished yet. She had a simple solution up her sleeve, one that had worked for her as long as she had owned the property. She came around the table to them, took Mykola and Olena by the hand, bent closer to them, and said that she believed that

God had brought them to her, she believed that they were the right people to take over, and she knew how to make it work.

Mykola and Olena looked at each other, took a few deep breaths, and implored her to continue. The answer was actually quite simple. Mykola and Olena, as owners, would choose one of the three apartments, whichever they liked the best. Isabella and Antonio would choose the next best, and renters would be found for the third floor because the current tenants were moving out shortly. Isabella and the third-ones would pay rent to Mykola and Olena, and it would be as simple as that.

Something puzzled Mykola. He took a moment to construct a question about a delicate matter. He asked Isabella why she would want to give up ownership of her three apartments, switching to renting and giving her money away to someone. With a sigh, Isabella countered that she was getting older and it was becoming more difficult for her to look after the place. She reasoned that income from the sale would carry her for a long time if properly invested. She had a few cousins who could advise her wisely. And eventually when Antonio got married and lived elsewhere with his wife, Isabella would move in with them and take care of their babies. When Isabella had a plan, it usually worked out her way.

The Attic

After Mykola and Olena moved out, life went on for Helena and Gregory in a sort of predictable way. The professor had moved out a long time ago, having met a local woman who eagerly took him in for love and money. They took some time getting used to having fewer people in their house, but they were both grateful that the noisy boys were gone and there was less thumping on the floor above their heads. The boys were entering their pre-teen years, their gangly legs and arms swinging into breakables too often. Now there were fewer things to find broken and hidden without apologies, and fewer things to repair.

Helena and Gregory converted their attic space into a proper bachelor apartment, removing a wall to make the space larger. They also added a rear metal entry and an outdoor fire escape. Their new tenant was a strange, very private woman named Daria, who never wore shoes up there and thankfully walked softly in stocking feet so no one would know if she was home or not. Only the slight creaking noise of the floor, which her ears didn't register, gave her away.

Daria's Plight

In her younger days, Daria studied hard and graduated with a medical degree, the only female in her class. For a short while, she worked in the local hospital gaining experience, aiming for a surgical specialty. But the war interfered with her plans and she was seconded to an army medical unit, far enough away from active warfare to be relatively safe but too close to her new supervisor, Dr. Natas Evila. He balked at having a woman in his unit, he took an immediate dislike to her, and he made no attempts to hide his opinion.

In a deliberate act of unkindness, Dr. Evila assigned Dr. Daria to a lowly team charged with bringing corpses from a battlefield to his makeshift mortuary. He took advantage of chaos and lack of oversight, and created his own primary objective, which was to study the bodies to observe and record the damage from shrapnel, bullets, and grenades. Later he would use his documented observations to profit wildly from designs for protective gear.

His secondary, cruel objective was to crush Dr. Daria, to make her leave by twisting the meaning of the assignment she had accepted. Where she understood that "responsible for the recovery of soldiers" meant caring for them and leading them back to health, Dr. Evila clarified in a lie that "recovery of soldiers" meant bringing them back dead.

She wouldn't last long. He was sure of it.

Dr. Daria was rightfully appalled and outraged. She could not reconcile how hauling bodies could be a job for a doctor and she felt completely tricked, but now she was forced to comply or risk charges of insubordination.

Travelling by truck into a battleground zone after an attack had subsided was a dangerous and unpredictable trip. They were subjected many times to nearby bombings and grenade explosions. Dr. Daria prayed that she and the men on the recovery team would have the luck and strength to live through this horrifying task, but several weeks into it, when she found an old high school classmate in a heap, partly blown away, her spirit and her heart finally broke.

Upon returning to the mortuary that night, she locked herself in a latrine and refused to come out. Before anyone could break down the door to force her out, she pulled a loose nail from the wall and frantically scratched Dr. Natas Evila's name into the wood of the latrine seat. There it would be nearly shat upon every day.

Daria's Discharge

When Dr. Daria refused to continue with the recovery team and spiraled into a depression, Dr. Evila recommended a psych discharge, and arranged her transfer to a Swiss health retreat to heal. He'd had some remorse about the way he treated her, and with that, he discovered that he had a conscience; sending her to Switzerland was an easy way to clear it.

She tried hard to put the various scenes of death out of her mind, but at night they snuck back in and played on the backs of her closed eyelids. After she left the retreat, it took several years for the movie-like projections that looped in her brain to subside. She tried to douse them with alcohol and various derivations of opiates, easily acquired in back alley dens.

As time went on, the movies played less often and with less intensity until she was mostly able to shut them out on her own without self-medicating. When she was finally able to completely free herself, she felt she had endured the hard climb of an unforgiving mountain. Dr. Evila's attempts to crush her had made her stronger, like soft coal becoming a hard diamond, the very opposite of what he intended.

There were two sides to Dr. Daria now. There was the strong-willed woman who could power her way through medical school, and later through depression and chemical dependence. And there was the reserved, cautious woman who tried to anticipate pitfalls before falling in head-first. Both sides were useful for survival. Both sides kept her afloat.

Daria's Arrival

When she arrived by boat in Halifax, she hoped the immigration doctor wouldn't notice that her hearing was impaired, damaged by battleground shells and rockets. Luckily he was only in it for the money and didn't really care one way or the other. He signed her entry papers and added her, and others, more than once to his payment ledger for invoicing, betting that no one would check his numbers and call him to audit his fees.

She worried forever that someone would find out. She hadn't declared her hearing problem upon entry to Canada and there were rumours that this could be grounds for deportation. But how could someone be deported to a country that didn't exist anymore? Where would she end up?

She decided to lay low and not attempt requalifying as a doctor. The process was too difficult and complicated for her anyway. Instead, she took a job as a midwife at a clinic in a poor part of Montreal, assisting with births and newborns to balance off her previous disastrous assignment with deaths. She worked until she frequently misunderstood or missed instructions, and she quit when she lost a forty-year-old mother giving birth to twins in breech. Leaving the room after that ordeal, in shock again, she missed hearing her colleagues say that it wasn't her fault.

Now that Daria wasn't working full-time, she lived off a small disability pension and the interest from an unexpected inheritance from her favourite aunt overseas. Daria lived a solitary, thrifty life, seldom integrating into her social surroundings except for necessities. She preferred the security of a half-hermit's routine. A daily newspaper, a pot of tea, a meal cooked to last more than one day. She did, however, venture out occasionally.

With no small amount of effort and resolve, she would make her way to the hospital's neonatal unit to donate a shoebox full of soft caps that she knitted. She liked going to peer in the viewing window of the newborns' nursery where she could see but not touch, somewhat like seeing kittens in the window of a pet store without having responsibility for their lives.

Daria's Revenge

While reading her morning newspaper, Daria remarked to herself with disgust—so many advertisements were creeping in and taking space from the more interesting content. She thought it should be called a "salespaper" because it was less about news and more about ad revenues and reaching into the population's pockets. She was quite happy without all the junk that was being pushed into people's homes.

Just as she was about to fold up the newspaper so it would fit in her small garbage can, she noticed an advertisement for something that piqued her interest. **Free Lecture**. It was sponsored by the Business faculty at the university nearby and was open to the public as part of an outreach program to engage members of the local community. But the speaker's photo was unsettlingly familiar and underneath it, his name blared loudly from the page even in small print.

Dr. Natas Evila.

Daria stared hard at the grainy picture, right into Natas' beady eyes, hoping his face would catch on fire. Her heart pumped harder and faster, and she broke out into a clammy sweat. It had taken her so long to forget him, but there he was again, uninvited, intruding in her home.

It took her not one second more to decide that she would attend the lecture coming up in three days. She would publicly confront the man who tried to destroy her, even if it killed her.

Daria's Apartment

The only people she spoke to besides shopkeepers and neonatal staff were Helena and Gregory, and rarely at that. She loved the attic apartment that she lived in and she made it an inviting, comfortable space with, unfortunately, no one to invite.

One day, Helena hadn't heard any creaking above her head and she hadn't heard Daria go clunking down the fire escape either, so she went upstairs and peered in the window to check. To her relief she could see Daria sitting at a small table, writing notes on a sheet of paper. She knocked, and then knocked again louder, getting Daria's attention, beckoning her to come to the door.

Because there was no vestibule to keep the cold wind out, Daria grabbed Helena by the hand and whipped her inside. Helena had never been in the apartment since Daria moved in. They were landlords who respected their tenants' privacy. Gregory had only been up there a few times for repairs, or so Helena thought, but he never commented on what he saw.

Helena stood dumbfounded. The apartment was basically one room, but Daria had hung multi-coloured Portuguese fabrics and sheets and Ukrainian scarves from hooks attached to the ceiling to make little billowy rooms, like she'd seen, she said, in the medical tents during the war. Here and there she hung some whimsical Portuguese Sardines, long stuffed fish made of cotton fabric. Daria had created an eccentric, jewel-toned palace in a box, a splendid room with variety and lightness.

Without asking why Helena had come, Daria put a kettle on an electric burner to make some tea. She motioned to

Helena to take a seat and since she was in no particular hurry, Helena sat. And then Daria sat.

They both sat. Awkwardly. Not having a hook to hang a conversation on.

The kettle squealed too loudly and a frazzled Daria took two quick steps to the kitchenette and began to prepare the tea with the formality of an experienced host. She returned to the table but was so excited to have a visitor that she knocked over the sugar bowl and apologized over and over again, in a happy, giddy sort of way.

Helena helped Daria clean up while sharing a story of her first dinner at her future in-laws' home. Still feeling embarrassed about it even now, she had spilled a dish full of hand-made perogies slathered in onions and butter onto the dining room table. From then on, the tablecloth retained the large stain and her mother-in-law, of course, retained the memory of the faux pas. Helena noticed the stain each time she came for dinner, and she finally took the hint and replaced it with a new one as a Christmas present.

Bonding over a spill, Helena and Daria talked for at least two hours more.

Near Miss

When Helena came back downstairs, Gregory was home, looking through the fridge for something to eat. She effused about Daria's lovely apartment décor and how they had a breakthrough and were now closer to possibly becoming friends. She described the hooks in the ceiling and the colourful partitions and the eccentricity of it all. Gregory muttered that it sounded nice and then left the room without the sandwich he had planned to make.

Preparation

Two days later, Daria was ready. After Helena left, she finished writing out notes of what she could remember from her terrible days under the thumb of Dr. Evila, and she had gone to the Main Library in search of information about his company. Mostly from news clippings and an article about his company in a trade magazine, she conceded that the ideas for his products were ingenious, but she saw no credit being given to the source of the data gathered to inspire the designs.

She took some time to remodel herself from her everyday look. She didn't want to look obviously like her normal self. She looped up her long, silver-blond hair into large curls and pinned them in a bundle on top of her head. She found the large, dark sunglasses that she wore when she thought she might feel too exposed. She unpacked a large third-hand Ocelot fur coat and aired it outside overnight to lose the smell of mothballs. She committed her concise revelations and her pointed question to memory, confident that they would spill out in the correct sequence. She found her way to the lecture hall and sat in the first row, left of centre and directly in front of the lectern.

The Dean of the Business faculty made a big fuss in introducing Dr. Evila and his accomplishments, and the audience clapped with enthusiasm as he rose up and settled in at the lectern, where he paused to unfold his notes. To make people feel appreciated for coming, he routinely scanned the full audience starting at the back of the room, although tonight he couldn't see a thing back there with the bright stage lights shining in his eyes.

As his gaze moved towards the front of the audience where he could make out the people in the first few rows, Daria noticed his slight hesitation when he scanned over her. Was it just her imagination? Was he surprised that someone would be wearing sunglasses indoors? Dr. Evila coughed a little, straightened his tie, and quickly rescanned the first row, cocking his head almost imperceptibly with a look of vague, out-of-context recognition.

Hookers and Hooks

The idea of putting up the hooks and partitions in Daria's apartment came from Gregory, inspired by the Parisian houses of ill repute into which he had slinked before heading home after the war. He suggested that she could get some colourful fabrics from the Portuguese shops along Boulevard St. Laurent. Daria thought it was a great idea and asked Gregory if he would help her screw and make sure everything was well-hung. He laughed at her little joke and slipped his arm around her waist, to which she did not recoil.

Although Daria had become somewhat agoraphobic, she had an easier time leaving her apartment when she had a clear purpose. She spent a few days hunting for and buying yards of lovely, colourful sheets of fabric, with lively colours and patterns, their diversity somehow working well together. She hadn't realized that Portuguese textiles were so vivid and alive. Seeing that Daria seemed very taken with the designs, the saleslady suggested adding a few handmade traditional Portuguese Sardines into the decorative mix. Daria bought seven of these stuffed cotton fish for good luck. She was sure she would need it some day.

At the last store she shopped at, a few steps down from sidewalk level, a Ukrainian woman rented a small space from Portuguese importers above. She sold bright and bold flower patterned scarves for the Sunday church-going babushkas. Some days her sales were very slow, so she was both overjoyed and horrified at selling most of her stock to Daria all at once. What would she have left to sell tomorrow?

Gregory had thoroughly enjoyed the creativity of hanging the sheets and scarves, but he had enjoyed Daria's quiet company as well. Each time he ventured back upstairs to get closer to completing the task, he enjoyed a little replay of Parisienne-like hospitality, getting closer to Daria in the bargain. He hoped that Daria and Helena would not become close friends. His simple tactic for not getting caught was to keep his head down and not over-visit his welcome. Out loud he would say to Helena, "I'm doing some repairing for Daria", but in his mind he snickered, "I'm doing some re-pairing *with* Daria". How fun it was to be sneaky.

Since they both snored loudly on and off during the night, neither Helena nor Gregory ever got a good sleep, each blaming the other, so Helena took to sleeping in Robert's old room. It always took her longer than Gregory to fall asleep. Under warm blankets that weren't being tugged, she could read with the light on until her eyelids grew heavy, and she could sleep and snore without waking Gregory and without getting poked in the ribs. For his part, Gregory had the gift of falling asleep almost immediately, and he was glad to have a little more room on the mattress, no frozen feet touching his legs, and visions of his wanderings playing out in his head.

Stomping

On this particular night, Helena and Gregory were both awoken by the sound of Daria hopping, dancing, laughing, and singing loudly upstairs. It was so out of character and so alarming that both of them threw on their housecoats and shoes, and ran up the fire escape to find out what in the world was going on.

Daria, still wearing the over-sized fur and sunglasses, with her curls now dislodged lopsidedly on her head, was beside herself with glee. When she stopped to catch her breath, she assured Helena and Gregory that she was alright. She was not having a breakdown or a stroke, and she was not drunk or high on drugs, but she was high as a kite on adrenaline and so, so happy.

Impressing Investors

Dr. Evila had learned over time that his favourite number was six. Distilling information to bites that could be easily chewed, his rather exuberant presentations described the six main features of his six most popular inventions, adding a teaser-preview of six future modifications that might be incorporated into his designs. His main motivation for giving presentations at all was to inform, to enthuse, and, ultimately, to sell products and attract investors.

He didn't see boredom or disengagement in the audience, except for one curiously impassive face under dark glasses in the front row. So he continued, outlining the manufacturing process and benefits to the economy, and stressing upon an individual's increased chance of surviving an attack. When he finally ended, he savoured a round of applause. The Dean, who had already purchased a fair number of shares a few years ago, complimented and thanked the speaker and invited questions from the audience.

Ambushed

A microphone had been set up on a stand in the centre aisle between rows one and two. Being an expert at turning each answer into a boast of his own genius, Natas deftly handled the questions that were soft-lobbed his way.

Until it was Daria's turn.

Daria stood up, walked to the microphone, took off her sunglasses, and looked straight at Natas. She asked him a simple question.

"You haven't mentioned how you gathered your data. Could you please elaborate?"

In an instant he figured out who she was, and he knew that she knew all about his methods. Still, it was a reasonable question, but when he attempted to answer, he hesitated and bumbled, and ventured into something convoluted and unprepared.

When he resorted to injecting lies and understatements, Daria took the microphone off the stand and turned to the audience, boldly revealing what he'd put her through, how he'd gathered the data, and the fact that all of his research was unauthorized. The product designs had sprung from tampering and desecrating bodies of dead soldiers, a heinous crime by all accounts.

She had to say this quickly and clearly, and she fully expected to be shouted down or removed, but instead, a pin was heard dropping in the room.

Natas smugly took the lack of reaction as a good sign. Then the crowd began to rumble and soon they were shouting at Natas, shouting that he was disgusting and cruel, and that his products carried a permanent stain and people should know. Someone even yelled at him, "You should be wearing your damned products now!"

Reported

An intern journalist for the university newspaper was madly scribbling notes of what she saw and heard. This lecture had turned out to be far more exciting than she had anticipated. She had never seen such a brilliant take-down before. The next day, Allison ran the story with her byline on the first page, and two days later it was picked up by a chain of national papers and spread across the land. Soon after that, her story was picked up by papers in the United States and Europe, and her career was cannon-launched.

Conversely and quite quickly, investors, including the Dean, withdrew support from Natas' business and drove it head-first into receivership. Natas still owned the patents and eventually rebuilt the business but took a silent partner role, which was difficult for his ego to swallow.

Many months later, Natas sat watching falling snow through the large, arched windows of his rented Westmount home. He was alone, sharing the evening with a tumbler of Crown Royal whisky. He thought about how Daria's concise question had so easily set his failure into motion. He imagined her sitting across from him now. Would she be gloating at her victory?

As one who enjoyed and benefitted from tripping up other people, he raised his glass to her in an in-absentia toast.

"Well-played," he acknowledged out loud.

Mykola and Olena's New Home

At Mykola and Olena's new home, they chose the ground floor apartment so they wouldn't have to use the steep and twisted stairs. They took their time selecting furniture that they could afford and they found some excellent second-hand shops where they bought utensils, dishes, and nearly new clothing.

Olena insisted on a set of brand new pots and a few sharp German knives, luxuries for the kitchen. Her beloved telephone was re-installed and placed on a small table by the window in the dining room corner nook. The dark mahogany table had a matching chair, whose upholstery would be well-worn into the future.

They were careful with their money, never made impulsive purchases, and waited to afford what they wanted. The boys were well-fed and clothed, and the mortgage payments were always made on time.

The boys were out most of the time with their friends, cooking up moneymaking schemes and learning wrong-headed facts about girls from each other. As long as they were home for dinner, no one really minded where they were. Olena continued working at the textile factory, having been promoted quickly to Supervisor on the sewing floor with a small office of her own, and she continued to make the arduous commute across town by bus.

Mykola moved up to managing three franchise stores owned by his boss. These stores were somewhat larger than a regular corner store and sold primarily food, drinks, tobacco, and magazines, and had a small rack of alcohol. One of the stores had opened on a street where it faced competition from a number of older establishments that always pretended to have sales and discounts, so Mykola needed to get creative to attract customers.

He knew he was in a neighbourhood of working-class immigrants who sent money and goods "back home" whenever they could, but the post office was far away and its opening hours were inconvenient. So Mykola came up with an idea. He ran a parcel sending service from a counter at the back of the store. The senders walked through the store past all the merchandise, and inevitably bought something on their way out.

This was a good deal for the store and a good deal for Mykola too, because the boss agreed that Mykola could keep a percentage of the profit from the service fees that he charged. Over time, as people grew familiar with Mykola's store and friendly service, more customers came, and the store began to stand on its own legs. This made the owner very happy as he watched the bottom line grow towards purchasing a fourth store. He wished he had more employees as sharp as Mykola.

Flashback

Right around closing time, Mykola was cleaning up and looking forward to going home. He was feeling very hungry and a little faint because he hadn't eaten enough that day. He never took anything off the shelf that he didn't pay for, and he had already spent his "extras budget" for that week. He just had to wait for the food that would be waiting for him at home.

A little bell hanging over the front door rang whenever someone came in or went out. Mykola heard the shrill little tinkle, a sound that he loved. It reminded him of the Celebration bell back home.

He watched as a new customer came into the store. Indeed, a new customer was always a cause for a small celebration.

The man looked perhaps a little shy with downcast eyes. His coat seemed somewhat too large and the sleeves were somewhat too long. He perused the shelves until he found the bag of flour he'd been sent out for, reaching out for it with his right hand.

Placing the flour on the front counter and treating himself to a chocolate bar from beside the cash register, he awkwardly gripped his wallet by squeezing it with his arm stump against his side while his good hand searched for the money.

Mykola felt the blood rush from his head and he saw sparks floating before his eyes. He steadied himself against the counter, hoping the man wouldn't notice his weakened state. Mykola hadn't thought about Lubomir's accident in a very long time. Seeing the customer one-handing the merchandise sparked a memory and sent Mykola back to a very bad day.

Landlords

Mykola and Olena's third-floor renters had turned over a few times and they increased the rent each time by a modest amount. The most current tenants were four American university students from wealthy families, justifying an even larger increase in rent. A muscular, bald man with a tattoo on his neck, across his Adam's Apple for god's sake, moved into the second-floor apartment after Antonio moved out to a bigger one nearby. He had gotten married and now had a baby girl, born "prematurely" as they told everyone. Isabella had moved in with them just as she had planned a long time ago.

Olena and Mykola missed having their good friends and easy tenants around, especially since the new man, Alphonse, nicknamed Alpha, had started to throw his weight around as if he owned the place.

Alpha complained about the parking. He took long showers and ran the shared water heater dry. He made unauthorized renovations while trying to bilk Mykola out of money by angrily waving faked receipts in his face. That went too far. Mykola and Alpha threw a few punches on the sidewalk, under the watchful eyes of the Polish lady leaning out of her window across the street. Her mouth gaped open at the unexpected action, and with an ill-timed sneeze, her top false teeth launched out into the air and down into the small garden space below.

Later as Mykola iced the side of his head, he admitted to Olena that the adrenaline rush was great and made him feel powerful, something he hadn't experienced before. Maybe he should pick a few more fights?

Olena laughed and suggested that he should go to the sparring gym a few blocks away to learn how to do it well instead of getting lucky and not losing any teeth. Perhaps the Polish lady had been a boxer in her younger days.

Hamilton

In Hamilton, Robert made good money, but as a shift-worker at the biggest steel company in the country, he was always tired. Nightshift was the worst for him. Between work, family, and caring for his home, he didn't have much time to travel to visit his parents Helena and Gregory, but he phoned them for short conversations almost every Sunday afternoon. Once a year in the summer, he loaded his family into the car and made the long drive to Montreal along Highway 2 to stay for a week with his parents. The kids loved to spend time with their grandparents, and with Mykola and his family coming over from their own home to visit, Helena and Gregory's house was filled to the brim again.

Visits Home

Helena and Gregory's living space was just over one thousand square feet, but in spite of its small dimensions it never felt small because the generosity with which it was offered was boundless. The pull-out couch in the spare room, the sofa in the living room, and cushions on the floor beside it were made up at night, and the thought of Robert and his children staying in a hotel never even entered into the conversation.

The green cracked ice Formica and chrome kitchen table became a work surface for the extra volume of food. Taking turns for the small bathroom, eating on unmatched plates in an otherwise formal dining room, and picking their way around their suitcases—those memories were bathed in a classic nostalgic glow. But it was the sound of laughter, or more serious consultations, or the blending of familial tones in old-country harmonies of soprano, alto, and bass after dinner, that resonated the most.

The blood relation between Mykola and Helena was never made exactly clear, but they were somehow related as cousins and that made their two families all related as well. Robert and his two daughters, Nicole and Karolina, would meet up with Mykola and Olena and their boys at Helena and Gregory's house, where there was a garden and outdoor patio area on the large corner property. Despite only spending short spurts of time with them, Robert's family got to know most of them quite well. With much of their visit occurring in the back yard, with sausages and burgers cooking on a charcoal grill, they would notice Daria clanking down the fire escape and slipping away down the driveway on her way to an errand. Without much more than a quick hello, she appeared shy or aloof. They weren't sure which.

Gregory's Garden

On a warm night when everyone had gone into the house to wrap up the evening, Mykola and Gregory stayed outside, primarily to avoid being asked to clean the kitchen, and mostly to enjoy some man-time without all the extra people around. Gregory had built a wooden garden swing and the two of them rocked gently, looking up at the few faint stars that could be seen. They felt totally relaxed after a long day of eating, drinking, and rousing discussions in which the adults talked over each other most of the time.

Mykola took a deep breath and blew it out, sounding exactly like a horse. It made Gregory laugh to see his nosy neighbour jump up to spy through her lace curtain. After a second or two, Gregory announced that he was very glad that Mykola had settled in Montreal. Their families got along and he felt a real kinship between them. With a slow nod of his head, Mykola agreed. He told Gregory that he and Olena were so grateful to them for helping them set their anchor in Canada and for everything they had done to help them as they settled. Who would have helped them in Argentina? No one. There was no real way to repay them and he was sorry he'd taken so long to really, really express his gratitude.

Gregory just nodded his head and kept rocking the swing. A long moment later, he said it was he who should show some gratitude because without Mykola's family, he and Helena would be quite alone most of the time.

Gregory continued talking about how proud he was of Mykola, a very decent, hard-working family man who obviously loved his wife and children, and did his best to adjust to a whole new world. Gregory hadn't spoken this much since Mykola met him, so he knew that Gregory's thoughts were deep and overflowing.

The more Gregory talked about family, the more Mykola's heart began to squeeze. It was a very strange feeling, one he'd experienced only twice before. And suddenly Mykola cracked. His face contorted, salty tears leaking down his cheeks, and when he regained his composure, he spoke in a hushed, private tone.

He begged Gregory to listen and not to judge him. He asked Gregory to press his right thumb against the bottom of his own sternum, to see how it felt, that heavy weight ever-present at the bottom of Mykola's heart. He made it clear that he hadn't told anyone else, including Olena, and his secret had been allowed to nag unchecked. By telling his story to someone he trusted, the invisible burden came to light and shrank away, but not quite completely.

Unrelated cousins turned into brothers on that swing, one a confessor, the other a confidant. As Gregory listened, he was reminded of his own secrets and chose not to share them at that time. The moment belonged to Mykola. Some other day, maybe next year, he would unburden himself. But not yet.

Helena's Loss

That fall, while tending to his dahlias, removing their tubers from the ground to prepare them for over-wintering, Gregory died from a brain aneurism right there in the garden. Helena didn't even know. She was busy canning late peaches and making plum jam, and her full attention was given to not scalding herself.

Having been drawn incidentally to her back window by the loud honking of migrating Canadian geese, Daria noticed Gregory lying motionless, facedown in the dirt. She flew down the fire escape and knocked frantically on Helena's back door before running out to the garden to help him, but she was clearly too late and clearly too distraught.

After a long period of mourning followed by a longer period of throwing out Gregory's old junk, Helena phoned Robert in Hamilton to ask if she could move in with him. Most of her few friends had either been moved to old-age homes or they had died. She didn't want to do either. She simply wanted to live closer to her son for her remaining days.

Nicole quite liked her grandmother Helena and tried to lobby for her, but Robert was used to his independence and distance from his mother, and needed some time to think about it. Selling her house and relocating the tenant would be a long-distance hassle for him for sure, and he wasn't certain how to handle it all.

Helena made short long-distance calls on several Sundays in a row to raise the stakes, first proposing that her pension cheques could be used to defray Robert's household expenses.

The following week, she called to remind him that she could still cook up a storm. Since his wife passed away, Robert had borne the brunt of many things domestic. Some help in the kitchen would definitely be a relief to him since neither Nicole nor Karolina had graduated from making grilled cheese sandwiches.

Yet another week, another phone call, and Helena pushed a little harder. She reminded him that he was her only son, and that she loved him and his children very much.

"Besides Robert, did you know that in Japan, all elders live with their families? It's just normal. Expected. If they can do it in their tiny apartments…" she trailed off.

In his mind, Robert was reaching for his wallet to buy her a plane ticket to Tokyo, but figured the Japanese had enough people of their own to worry about.

He eventually conceded the benefits of having Helena with them, but he still resisted because of all the work that would have to be done. He would have to sell her house in Montreal. He would have to make his house senior-friendly by installing things like handrails in the bathroom, maybe even converting the main floor den into a room for Helena so she wouldn't have to climb the stairs. And what would she do in the house all day? Robert would have to research the senior centres in his area to see what outings and services they provided. His tendency to over-think things took up more time than it would have taken to just get on with it.

Nicole reasoned with him that he would have the house-selling hassles eventually whether Helena came or not. Robert was clearly in some sort of a funk, spending more time hammering something in the garage, and she wasn't sure what it would take to throw him over.

Her Own Phone

A few days after Helena's last call, Nicole answered the new phone in her own upstairs bedroom. The telephone company had recently run a summer-job-creating promotion to install extra phone jacks for free. This created hundreds of jobs for university students who happily, and somewhat haphazardly, ran cables all through people's houses, through walls, over door casings, and along baseboards to whichever rooms the clients desired.

Nicole's room got a jack, of course, but Karolina was the only kid on the planet who didn't want one. Answering the phone just wasn't her thing, and she never bothered to get up from whatever she was doing anyway, especially if a bag of chips was involved. Robert always knew that Nicole would answer the phone if she were home, so he mostly left it to her to screen any calls.

"Olena's calling!" Nicole shouted down the stairs.

Robert lifted the receiver from the phone attached to the kitchen wall, its cord long enough for him to sit at the kitchen table. Having spent some time with Helena, sifting through Gregory's belongings and reducing their joint clutter, Olena learned that Helena wanted to move. Although she was very sad to hear this news, Olena wanted Robert to know that they should do whatever would be best for Helena, but if she did move, Olena would miss her very much. Her only stipulation was that their families should continue to visit once a year and come to her home where she and Mykola would be very happy to host them.

Robert assured her that he had no intention of giving up on trips to Montreal. He loved it there and it was good to get everyone together. He just wasn't able to make a plan for Helena yet. He really wasn't the impulsive type so a solid plan was necessary for him to proceed. He wasn't quite sure when it would come about, but he was working on it.

Olena hung up the phone, satisfied, knowing that the seed had been sown.

Sometimes a Miracle

Another three months passed without a plan, but during this time Helena confided in Daria that she needed to sell the house because she just couldn't carry it financially anymore. The final cost of Gregory's unexpected funeral caught her by surprise and sucked her rainy day bank account dry. She wanted to find the right buyer, someone who would allow Daria to stay in the attic if she wanted.

Helena had already been approached several times by strangers looking to buy her house but who blew any chance at a deal by making ridiculously low offers. She was wise and very wary of being taken advantage of, and not in a rabid rush. It had to be the right person, someone with the right motivation and integrity and a good, solid offer. She needed a miracle.

As it turned out, Daria had a referral—her very own miraculous boyfriend, Stanley, who was an expert in acquiring real estate at good prices.

The Crush

Daria met Stanley at Gregory's funeral home visitation. Stanley was the funeral home director and he knew all about Helena being a widow stuck with a house and no family nearby. He'd heard her talking about maybe wanting to move to Hamilton, but the house was like an anchor around her waist and she didn't want to displace her tenant, Daria, from her home.

Stanley owned various properties around the city and credited the Monopoly game for teaching him acquisition strategies in his youth. He had a steady stream of widows coming to his office almost every day, so he was choosy regarding the properties that he sought out for his personal portfolio. Helena's home was on a prime piece of real estate that could easily be rented out or redeveloped later, and so, Stanley began his pursuit by laying low in the bushes, gaining trust, and waiting for Helena to fly into his web.

At first, Stanley wondered why the woman standing by Gregory's casket was staring at him. His assistant noticed too and joked that, oh ho, Stanley had an admirer. Daria had the good looks of a woman who must have been a knock-out in her younger days, but she turned her head and blushed whenever Stanley met her eyes. She hadn't experienced a crush since she was sixteen years old and it felt great, with magical chemicals shooting around inside her body. But the half-hermit was shy and kept her distance.

Stanley watched Helena as she called out across the room, "Daria, thank you for bringing the donuts. That was very kind of you!"

And that's when he realized that the shy lady was the tenant that Helena didn't want to force out when she sold her house.

There was a small refreshment bar set up in the room on the opposite side from Gregory's casket. When Daria went over there to get a drink, Stanley followed. In his head, he had a plan to ask Helena if he could buy her house, but he hadn't considered the bonus of a potential girlfriend as part of the bargain.

Stanley wasn't married anymore and didn't have any human children, but his real estate holdings required care and attention and had personalities of their own, so he felt like they were part of his family. A real, live girlfriend would be so much better, he thought.

He asked Daria if she would have dinner with him at an Italian restaurant not far from the funeral home. Without hesitation and a little over-enthusiastically, she said yes.

Over the course of a few months, they got to know each other quite well, and when Helena brought up the subject, Daria put in a good word for Stanley. She felt he was an honest man who worked hard at increasing his real estate holdings. He had been quite upfront with his hopes and plans, and he assured Daria that she could keep living happily in her eccentric hovel, or maybe she might one day consider moving in with him.

The Catch

Soon a sales contract was drawn up with terms and conditions made agreeable to Helena, and Stanley became the new owner of her house. He was very good at biding his time, reeling in the fish. Everything was done legally and aboveboard because he didn't want anyone to suspect him of taking advantage of his funeral home clients. And really, if one stopped to think about it, he was just offering another great service, since the widows were able to exchange a burden and a headache for a nice bundle of cash.

Helena was never under any real obligation to Daria, and had she known about her involvement with Gregory, Helena wouldn't have given Daria's welfare a second thought.

Dr. Daria would have been quite capable of checking the damage of the boot-shaped bruise on her ass. But as it were, Helena rested well knowing that Daria could continue to live in the attic apartment uninterrupted until she herself made the choice to move elsewhere.

I'm Here

Not long after the sale of her home, Helena clambered into a taxi at the Hamilton train station. The driver was nice enough to help her ease into the seat, offering to assist her with the seatbelt.

"Letta me help you," he said, with a strong Italian accent. "You reminda me of my mama."

He smelled strongly of cigar smoke and lightly of beer, but there were no other drivers at the taxi stand to choose from. In spite of what she would describe as a "Chicago Ride", Helena arrived on her only son's doorstep in one piece. She placed her two suitcases beside her on the front porch and rang the doorbell.

Robert opened his front door.

"What the hell?" is how he greeted his mother.

Still catching her breath from the romping ride through the green synchronized lights all the way down Main Street, Helena stated matter-of-factly, "Be happy. I sold the house myself. I took care of all the details so now you don't have to. Just take care of me."

Robert gave her a big hug, brought her inside, and called out to the girls.

"Hey, come on down. Look who's here!"

Robert and the girls quickly set up Helena in the spare room upstairs. None of them could quite believe that she had actually come the whole distance on her own. When Robert apologized for not having installed bathroom handrails, Helena scowled and complained.

"You're crazy. Those things are for old people. What's next, a walker?"

Naturally, it was a bit rough at first, with everyone discovering that the long-haul was more difficult than a short-stay vacation. They all tried to adjust to conflicts over well-ingrained and often opposing routines. There was a radio in Helena's room that she'd taken to blaring unbearably loudly. Back at her Montreal house, Daria had never complained. Sometimes Daria's hearing impairment served Helena well.

Summer Trips

They continued to make their annual summer treks to Montreal, with Helena in the back seat. They brought extra pillows because the humming sound of both the engine and the rubber meeting the road, and the warmth on the back of her head from the sun, would invariably put her into a car-coma. Over time, the highway became wider, their latest car had more horsepower, and the roadside rest stops were vastly improved. They knew when they crossed the Ontario-Quebec border because the highway got bumpy, and soon, predictably, Robert would joke that they still hadn't fixed the spelling mistakes in "St. Télesphore".

Now, instead of heading to Helena and Gregory's old house, Olena had seamlessly taken over the role of hosting them because that's what family does, and that's what made her happy.

Olena eagerly transferred the dates of the family visit from one calendar to the next, written in ink and expectation. Each year before they arrived, Olena worked to stuff the freezer with food to warm up later, packed the fridge with containers and fresh vegetables, and loaded the groaning cupboards with extra supplies for the arriving guests. No one ever left Olena's without putting on pounds, bursting with laughter, and planning the next visit "home".

Street-Wise

Robert's daughters always wanted to hang out with Olena's boys when they came to Montreal because Marko and Peter were a few years older and light-years more street-wise and cooler than Nicole and Karolina felt. The boys tolerated them to some degree, usually only at family meal times, but then, as quick as a slingshot pellet, they were out the door and in the wind, up to who-knows-what.

When they weren't doing something with the family, like visiting Beaver Lake or driving to gawk at the mansions in Westmount, Nicole and Karolina were left to amuse themselves by wandering around the neighbourhood, finding interesting junk in alleys, or stopping for ice cream at a corner Dépanneur.

They saw children as young as eleven years old smoking cigarettes in a playground. They were whistled at by older men driving past them in rumbling cars. Once, they stood in horror on the sidewalk, listening to a man inside an upstairs apartment swearing and beating his wife for not having dinner ready on time. They regretted wanting to be more what they thought of as "street-wise" because so far that wasn't any fun, but they still wondered what Marko and Peter did when they weren't around.

Chinatown

When the boys were heading out again after dinner, Marko nudged Peter who asked the girls if they wanted to come along. This was a big surprise. Nicole and Karolina jumped at the chance to be included in something that had to be more exciting than sitting around the house while the adults talked and talked. Olena had noticed that the boys were ignoring the girls most of the time and she suggested that they be nice and do something fun with them. She gave them twenty dollars for a movie downtown. That would be nice.

The four of them left the house and walked over to the main street bus stop. As soon as the bus pulled up, the boys scooted in through the rear door, dragging the girls with them and not paying for the ride. This was how cool kids got around. The bus driver knew these boys and since they seemed to be showing off to their new girlfriends, he decided to ignore them. He didn't need any more confrontations that night.

Looking out the bus window, Nicole spied the neon lights of the theatre marquee in the distance. She asked Marko what movie they were going to see, but he just scoffed and rolled his eyes at Peter.

"Uncle Nick's, right?" whispered Peter.

"Yup," confirmed Marko.

The bus rolled on past the theatre and took a turn down to the old part of town. Soon they were in Chinatown, something the girls had never seen before. The closest they'd ever come to something like that in Hamilton was the old Rickshaw restaurant, with its red paper lanterns, carved dragon wall decorations, Chinese banners with no translations, and a curious array of misplaced Polynesian artifacts. To Nicole and Karolina, Montreal's Chinatown was like being in another country altogether.

Detour

They popped out of the bus with the girls following the boys for about five minutes until they reached the front of the Sun Moon Authentic Chinese Food Diner. The smell of wok oil wafted to the street and Nicole heard her stomach rumble. She was about to reach for the door when Marko clicked his tongue and tossed his head in the direction of the tight alley next to the building. Nicole looked to Karolina for agreement, and they both followed Marko to a back door that had suffered its share of kicks and dents, its window covered in wire security mesh, but was, strangely, left unlocked.

Inside, they followed a narrow staircase down to a metal door. Peter knocked in a coded pattern and a small Asian man, who was round like a snowman, opened the door. Clearly, he knew Peter and Marko, and only looked a little concerned about the new girls coming in, probably because they were all underage, but he let them in because they weren't the first ones that the boys had ever brought downstairs.

Nicole and Karolina's eyes were wide with caution and they both had an uneasy feeling. What went on in this place? The large room was half-dark and windowless. To their left, there was a long bar with a worn-out counter top with beer taps, and many different liquor bottles lined up on the shelves behind it. A thin man, who was tall enough to reach the top shelf, was pouring mixed drinks in fluid, decisive motions.

Towards the back of the room, there were three pool tables, two poker tables, and through the smoky haze, they could see a pinball machine where a young, greasy punk was taking out his game-over anger by kicking its legs and slamming its sides.

Out of nowhere, Uncle Nick lunged over to the punk and knocked his leg out hard from under him. He swore that if the kid ever kicked his machine again, he'd lay him out and crack his head. Punks have no respect.

Marko shook Uncle Nick's enormous hand, gave him a quick man-hug, and introduced him to his cousins. Nicole and Karolina noticed his swarthy Romanian looks and his thin pencil moustache, an attempt at channeling Clark Gable without giving a damn about anything.

For as long as Marko could remember, he felt closer to Uncle Nick than to his own father. Uncle Nick never turned away any young person from his establishment, even if it meant risking the odd raid or two. He would rather have them in his sight than getting into trouble on the streets. To the kids, he was like that family friend that's called "Uncle" even though he's not related. He had been a small-time thief in his younger days, and being adept at nicking stuff without getting caught, "Nick" became his alias. No one knew his real name.

Peter asked if they could order some food from upstairs. When the sweet and sour chicken, eggrolls, and chow mein arrived, there were no forks. Marko grabbed chopsticks for the four of them from a jar on the bar and started plucking food straight out of the containers. Marko made a slurping sound as he sucked in the chow mein. Nicole and Karolina looked at each other and burst into laughter. They hadn't a clue of how to hold chopsticks properly, so Peter showed them patiently while Marko kept eating. He was a bit of a bastard that way.

By the time the girls got the hang of using the chopsticks, Marko had had enough food, actually most of it. Peter ordered more, and then smashed an eggroll into Marko's face. Pig. Luckily this pig thought it was funny. Nevertheless, he plotted his revenge, reserving it for sometime in the future when it would be least expected.

Marko motioned to the bartender, holding up four fingers. Four draft beers arrived at their table, no questions asked, no ID shown. The girls, trying to be cool, reached for the beer and drank. Nicole had snuck beer in small amounts ever since she was little, drinking from stale glasses or bottles left behind at family parties. Not surprisingly, she liked the fresh draft much better.

Karolina still didn't have a taste for beer and turned up her nose, but remembering that she should act cool, she drank some and pretended to like it. But, actually, she hated it. She wondered how it was possible for beer to be so popular when she could barely get past the first sip. She wondered if being an adult meant faking it some of the time.

Marko Plays

Since Marko finished eating before them, he strutted over to the pool table and called out loudly to a man who he seemed to know, enticing him to play. Marko moved with confidence and practised grace, sinking a few balls in a row with carefully planned and placed shots.

When he accidently sunk the cue ball, his face changed to an angry red colour and he got really quiet, his movements more reserved as if he were storing up energy to go for the kill. In the end, the other player made several mistakes and Marko won, but there was nothing satisfying in it for him. No money exchanged hands. It was more like a gentleman's game with less drama, less show. Too easy.

He didn't want to pick a fight with anyone tonight, not in front of his cousins.

Time to Go

Before it got too late, Peter got them moving on their way back to the house. He felt that he and Marko had included the girls enough and they had taught them some new things. The only little problem now was that they knew too much about where the boys hung out. Peter could tell that the girls had gotten a good thrill by experiencing the underworld for a bit. The boys promised that if the girls didn't tell the truth about what they'd seen or heard or did that night, they would bring them back to Uncle Nick's again next year as a reward.

Nicole was feeling a little light-headed and queasy. It couldn't have been just from the beer because she didn't even finish her glass. It might have been the food, fried in week-old wok oil that should have been refreshed three times by then. There were some men in the corner at the poker table heaving on French cigarettes, which probably did the trick. The smoke made her and Karolina feel nauseous and they couldn't wait to run up the stairs and out into the fresh air of the alley, only to be bombarded by the smell of rotting fish and meat in a dumpster that had been pushed out for collection. Then when the bus pulled up, belching thick, black, diesel smoke, that did it. Nicole bent over and threw up beside a nearby bush. The other three kept their distance until she stood up again, reaching into her little purse for a tissue and a stick of gum, offering some to Karolina. Peppermint in any form always made them feel better.

Smooth Liar

The adults were cleaning up when the kids got home and there was no way for the youngsters to avoid them to get to their beds. Olena's sense of smell was finely tuned and she knew from the doorstep that they'd been up to no good.

She asked Karolina, the youngest and most liable to tell the truth, if they had enjoyed the movie, but Karolina hesitated, still not feeling quite normal. Marko spoke up, lying that the movie was fine but because there were so many people smoking in the theatre, they left partway through and went to an ice cream parlour instead.

"That's why Nicole and Karolina look so sick. They ate way too much. You should have seen them pile on the whipped cream and chocolate sauce, the works!" invented Marko. Nicole and Karolina couldn't help being impressed by how easily Marko could pile it on himself.

All four delinquents announced that they were headed to bed. Olena wished them a good sleep, not wanting to make a scene right then. She glanced at Mykola but he was oblivious, as usual, when it came to their boys.

At the Cabin

The large, deluxe log cabin on Lac McTuque belonged to Isabella's rich lawyer cousin. It had three separate spokes radiating from a central hub with its grand stone fireplace. Two of the spokes contained bedrooms and the third had the kitchen and common areas. His grandfather had purchased the property for peanuts through an auction years ago, and developed it into a family compound that they all enjoyed.

Their large Italian family gathered there every summer, and Isabella and Antonio joined them for a week while Olena and Mykola had visitors. Cousins, aunts, and uncles amused themselves by driving boats and waterskiing on the lake, playing bocce on the large back lawn, or driving golf balls into the lake from a tee box near the shore. Some just sat wearing cut-off shorts and tie-dyed t-shirts or Moo-Moo dresses in large comfortable wicker chairs, absorbing sunlight and spiked lemonade.

The only price they were each expected to pay was one full day's worth of light summer maintenance, such as cutting grass, painting railings, cleaning the shore line, or pruning overgrowth. They did it happily to pay back the generosity of the free food and board, and to be invited back next year.

Except one of them. Cousin Domenic complained that he was doing more than the rest, when it was known that he was actually doing less. His whining and ungratefulness got him uninvited for several years until he groveled his way back, accepting several days' worth of work as a punishment.

He'd grown up and matured, and wasn't such a big, weasily baby anymore. Isabella wouldn't have put up with his nonsense if he had been her son, but her sister thought he walked on water. Antonio had once pushed Domenic out of the boat into the lake to prove that wasn't true.

At night, they would gather around a large bonfire and sing or talk, or just stare into the leaping tongues. As the fire eased off to glowing embers, it was time to go to bed. No one ever complained about going to bed, not even the youngest, because after a full day of exercise and fresh air, the quality of deep, relaxing sleep was the absolute best.

With city lights far away, the natural darkness crept in as the sun set behind a mountainous rise to the west and soon the moon's glow lit up a shimmering streak across the lake. Someone in the group would start a chain of contagious yawning and off they'd go, usually feeling sleepy by only nine-thirty in the evening.

Over time, the family kept growing with more marriages and births than deaths. Before and after his marriage, the cousins teased Antonio gently about not having a girlfriend.

"Hey Antonio, should we invite Cornelia from the German family next door?"

"Or maybe Geneviève from the bakery. Her strong arms could give you a good massage."

Antonio always laughed and replied that he had a girlfriend back home. His family thought he was making a joke.

Chapter 4

In the Meantime 1955–1963

Daydreams

Olena's bus stopped in front of Madame Laflamme's Ballet Studio on Boulevard St. Laurent. In the afternoon when she got off, she would often land right into a gaggle of little girls with tight buns on their heads, wearing pink leotards. They were heading into the studio for a scheduled class of technique or rehearsal or exam preparation. By the happy chattering amongst them, it was obvious that they enjoyed Madame Laflamme's steady encouragement and careful guidance of their physical and skill development. All hopes and toes were pointed towards illustrious careers on a European stage but, more likely, settled for walking gracefully and confidently, no matter what they encountered.

When Olena was a young girl, her mother took her to see a performance by a travelling ballet troupe from the self-renowned Mudra-Baba Academy. It was a rather amateur production, sloppy to the trained eye, but to Olena, it was the most beautiful piece of performance art she had seen as a child. Later, she couldn't recall where they were from or what production they were trying hard to convey, but she was left with a lasting impression of the girls on the stage moving lightly like butterflies or spinning like inexhaustible tops, or grouping, regrouping, twining, untwining, circling, leaping, and emoting with their entire lithe beings.

Olena's mother had not anticipated the effect. She rebuffed Olena's constant pleading to become a ballet dancer, knowing they had neither the money nor the time for such a privileged indulgence. No matter how much Olena cried, her mother's answer was always "Noh". Later in life, Olena guessed that this was why her innate reaction to new ideas was usually "Noh" as well.

Occasionally, Olena allowed herself a few minutes to decompress after getting off the bus. She stood at the ballet studio window off to one side, watching the girls warm up at the barre. With a quick hand-clapping by Madame, the girls fell into line formation, ready and attentive. Olena wished her boys were more like these girls in that regard.

Olena loved shopping at the Marché du Nord. The large and abundant year-round displays of fruits and vegetables reminded her of harvest time back home but without all the hard work.

Bumping into Madame Laflamme at the tomato stand was an unexpected surprise. She was dressed more elegantly than when she was teaching in class, and her hair was combed back into a perfect French twist instead of a bun. Madame looked up at Olena with an inquiring look on her face.

"Excuse me, you look familiar. Ah, you're the woman who watches my studio. Am I right? Were you ever a dancer yourself?"

"Oh, noh. My mother wouldn't let me, but I really wanted to be. It's too late for me to start now", Olena said knowingly.

Madame replied kindly, "Well, actually, yes. To be excellent at ballet requires years of training best started at a young age."

"Yes, I'm sure that's how it works. But one can still dream," Olena countered wistfully while filling her basket.

Madame agreed. "Certainly. One always should dream."

A few weeks later, Olena got off at her usual stop in front of the studio, but there were no girls that day. The studio was closed and the lights were off. Some sort of holiday closure, perhaps? Something on the doorknob caught her eye and being curious, Olena went to see what it was. There, taped to the glass door was a printed note saying, "Madame Laflamme announces her retirement. The studio is now permanently closed. Thank you to all of you who made my life fuller, and good luck."

Tied to the doorknob was a bag and attached to the bag was a hand-written note, "For the lady I spoke with at the market. The lady who watches through the window. Lightly used, from me to you. They will help you dream."

Olena untied the bag from the doorknob and pulled the drawstring open. Inside was something that gripped her and made her nose sting from impending tears. The bag contained a pair of clean and perfect pink pointe shoes, larger than a child's size. Lightly used. From Madame to her. Except for the satin ribbons that she would later tie around her ankles, there were no strings attached.

At the Factory

Most days at the textile factory ran smoothly, with the exception of a spat or two between women who had worked too closely together for too long. Words were used as weapons that left no visible trace because they knew that crimes with scissors could lead to deportations. It was a good thing that the sewing machines were too heavy to throw because sometimes it was just that bad.

Today, perhaps because it was just before a full moon, everything seemed to be going wrong. Two sewing machines had broken down, the fuse for the cooling fan had blown, and a new, inexperienced man had been hired to the maintenance crew. Olena couldn't help but wonder how a brand new employee would deal with fixing machines under a time-crunch. Every minute wasted by broken machines caused misery in the accountant's office. He, in turn, was able to cast a shroud of panic on everyone to dissipate his own anxiety, leaving Olena to settle everyone back down again.

Olena waited for the repairman to show up so she could point him in the right direction to the broken machines. A few moments later, looking up from her daily planning sheet, she saw the new man standing with his back to her, speaking to the maintenance boss. There was something about the way he tilted from left to right that looked familiar. It took her a second to realize that it was Antonio! She hadn't expected him at all, and as he turned and approached her office door, she jumped up to greet him. He smiled shyly and only said, "I am here to fix."

Olena gave Antonio a big, hearty hug that lasted a little too long, setting off whispers on the sewing floor, and the smell of her warm skin made Antonio pull out a mental yellow card on himself. He was mindful of being a married man, but a hug from Olena, a simple pleasure, was something he liked very much. He'd wished for something like that from the moment he met her at the negotiation, and he hadn't expected it to happen today. He felt a little embarrassed at thinking like a schoolboy, so without saying much, he set to work on the machines she'd pointed out and within a half hour each, got them going again.

In the lunchroom, Olena was taking her break, peeking into her food bag. Mykola had made her a nice sandwich with fresh bread and ham from the store, with a juicy whole tomato, and a piece of apple pie from yesterday's sale at Praszek's down the street. Antonio slid down the bench to sit in front of her and ate his lunch in his usual quiet state. He didn't realize the chance he was taking when he commented that she looked tired. Normally when a woman is told that she looks tired, she doesn't react happily. But instead of cutting him to the bone, Olena blamed it on her long commute, on having to get up so early, on getting home so late, adding with a laugh that she never got enough sleep to restore her natural beauty. Antonio pushed up his bottom lip and his eyebrows and nodded, and when he finished eating, he slid off the bench to take on more chores, proving himself to his new boss.

Commute Commuted

A week later when the end-of-day bell rang, all the factory workers rose from their places and headed for the door. Olena had had another long day with problems arising from feuding co-workers and late out-going fabric shipments. She had a headache and her ankles were swollen, and now she had to face the long commute back home. She would probably have to stand in the bus aisle because she was on the younger side of the passengers and no one would think to give up their seat for her. She packed up her things and was locking up her filing cabinet when she was startled by Antonio who appeared silently at her office door.

"I bought a car", he declared. And then, as naturally as could be, Antonio and Olena began a routine that lasted over twenty-five years. He picked her up in the morning and drove her home at night. He never asked her for any gas money because he was going to work anyway, and she was paying him, so to speak, just by being with him. They rarely had a real conversation, mainly hello, goodbye, and thank you's on both ends. This suited them very well because he never talked much anyway, and Olena was usually short on sleep on the way in and headachy-tired on the way out.

Mykola wondered about the driving. The women at work wondered about the driving. Isabella wondered about the driving. But Olena insisted that it was just that. Nothing. And Antonio, as usual, said nothing about it at all.

She Gone

Without any warning, Antonio's wife took the children and moved out. She didn't like that Antonio washed and polished the car frequently in which he drove Olena, but he never lifted a finger to help her in their home. She'd heard two women gossiping about it in the dairy aisle, two old cows having a laugh over what must go on in that car. She moved back in with her parents who drove her crazy, but at least they had conversations and arguments like normal people. She couldn't take Antonio's taciturn ways any more, always having to guess what he was thinking and what he was doing, which really couldn't have been so difficult.

After Antonio's wife left him, Olena and Mykola invited him and Isabella to join them and Helena and Gregory for high-holiday meals, Christmas, then Easter, where they shared in delicious feasts, and where Isabella did more than enough talking for the eight of them. Antonio would occasionally speak up to ask for something on the table but never in opinion or complaint or concern. Olena had gotten very good at reading his facial expressions, and she and Isabella, but luckily not Mykola, had figured out long ago that Antonio had a secret that he thought he'd kept well-hidden.

Alpha Over and Out

On a hot, humid, and breezeless Saturday evening, Mykola and Olena were putting away some groceries bought earlier in the day and were cleaning up their little kitchen. It was shortly after ten o'clock at night and it had been dark outside for nearly an hour already. Their kitchen door was open to let in some cooler night air, along with some large moths attracted to the light. The door led to their back garden and parking area, which was accessed from a narrow alley that ran the length of the block.

They could hear someone's radio booming with a late-night baseball game's announcer's voice, a neighbour's son practising his saxophone imagining himself a great musician, and another neighbour's cat yowling from the pain that saxophone caused. The two upper apartments' kitchens had doors opening to balconies that ran along the back half of the apartment to the fire escape addition, the stairs of which were ironically made of tinder-dry wooden planks, the walls of which would have acted as a chimney. Modern building codes would not have permitted such a structure, but there were thousands of them in the city and insurance companies probably loved them for creating exclusions in the fine, fine print.

They could hear Alpha thumping around upstairs and furniture being shoved roughly across the floor. There was some shouting with several male voices in the heat of an argument. Who knew what it was this time? A debt unsettled, a drug deal gone bad, a woman being fought over? It was uncomfortable but entrancing to listen in, and these fights normally blew over as quickly as they started.

But this time as an angrily shouting man ran out onto the balcony of the apartment above, Mykola and Olena froze to try to understand what was happening. The shouting got louder and more urgent. More voices.

"You rat bastard, I'll set your place on fire! Marcello, bring the gas!"

They realized that the small mob was running towards the back stairs. These were locals speaking English with Montreal accents; they knew the stairs would be easy to set ablaze.

Alpha struggled briefly with one or two of the men. It was hard to tell how many. They grunted and grappled, and suddenly a cracking sound was followed by a dull thud. A second or two later, the sound of feet running back into the apartment and the distant sound of footsteps fleeing down the outdoor staircase left a wake of eerie silence.

Mykola and Olena listened, still frozen, until they were sure the men were gone. Then they ran out of their kitchen door to see what had happened. It was immediately obvious that it had been the balcony's wooden railing that had cracked and broken, some of it dangling from above like an arrow pointing to a crime. They had already guessed what had happened. There, a little further over, was a very still Alpha, sprawled out on the ground, his head bent unnaturally. His body was pierced in several places by rebar rods from an unfinished cinderblock garden retainer, one of the projects for which he had tried to overcharge Mykola.

"Holy mother of god, what do we do now?!" exclaimed Olena.

She ran to get a sheet and Mykola spread it over Alpha and the rebar so the children wouldn't see his body if they woke up. Olena called the police to report the situation, calling it an accident because she didn't want them to investigate further and cause problems for them with the thugs.

The police smelled the alcohol wafting off Alpha's body and chalked it up to a drunken mishap. Mykola had poured a little extra onto Alpha's shirt just so there would be no mistake.

Alpha was "known to police" and they had considered it only a matter of time before he got himself killed. Good riddance. One of the officers remarked that falling off a balcony seemed like a silly way for him to die; a blaze of bullets would have been more fitting for a guy from Kingston Pen.

Finding out that they had rented an apartment to a convicted criminal was very disconcerting. They knew Alpha wasn't a boy scout, for sure, but they didn't know that he had actually done time. In Kingston Penitentiary, no less. Olena and Mykola had overlooked Alpha's red flags because he had flashed his cash, but they would be more careful with future tenants from now on. They would pay more attention to their instincts because getting the truth was much harder to do.

Luckily the boys had gone to bed early and never saw Alpha's body before it was taken away. They didn't hear the faint sucking sound as his lung slipped off one of the steel bars. They slept through the whole event and in the morning they were only told that Mr. Alphonse had died in an accident. They didn't need to know that they had come so close to danger. If those men had managed to set the fire, it would have been a disaster.

That night, Mykola and Olena lay in bed too awake to sleep. The event had shaken them, especially the threat of setting a fire that would have put them and possibly the whole block in danger. Mykola noted that he should check their insurance policy to make sure they would be covered if anything bad like that ever happened. Working at the store, he had overheard customers complaining of getting worked over by insurance companies and reaching settlements they felt were way below their expectations. There was also something about depreciation that he didn't quite yet understand.

As his eyelids grew heavy, Mykola asked Olena if it was wrong that he felt relieved that it was the end of Alpha, but she replied fervently with her recently acquired rude-English expressions.

"That son-a-fabitch got what he deserved and I'm so glad he's gone. He was mean and a self-centered, drunken bastard, and the world doesn't need people like that."

She felt better just by saying it out loud.

Mykola agreed and gave her a good night kiss. After talking the evening's events through and coming to the conclusion that they didn't feel sorry for Alpha at all, they fell into a deep, restorative post-adrenaline sleep.

When the alarm went off only a few hours later, Olena felt more awake than when she tried to get a full night's sleep. She quickly smacked the alarm button, uncoiled herself from a fetal position stretching her arms and legs, rubbed her eyes, and rolled out of bed. Maybe she would need a nap when she got home, but for now, it was a good start.

She shuffled to the bathroom and then to the kitchen, and as she started to make her coffee, a terrible realization flashed through her brain. She turned to go to Mykola, but he was already standing in the kitchen doorway, with the same alert urgent look on his face. They had been so focused and happy about not having to deal with Alpha anymore that they hadn't made the connection—now there was no tenant to pay the rent. No rent, no mortgage payment. The son-a-fabitch was still causing trouble for them even after death.

Cleaning Up

Alpha's ex-wife and his sister came to clean out the apartment a few days after the elaborate church funeral during which much effort was put in to create the impression that Alpha was a saint among saints. Those who knew better played along in case he was watching from above and out of respect for his mother. His mother thought her son had been born an angel, and although that might have been correct at the moment of birth, the effect didn't last long.

Willfully oblivious, his mother had played a big role in creating this monster. She allowed Alphonse to do whatever he wanted, believing his lies, and turning a blind eye to his criminal behaviours, that began even when he was just a cherub. All he had to do was call her "ma très belle maman" or something easy like that, and she would always look the other way.

There wasn't much left to throw out since his ex-wife had taken most of the good pieces when she left him. Still, she and his sister hoped to find something of value stashed away. They had agreed in advance to split any findings fifty-fifty, swearing on their mothers' graves. But that agreement depended on who found what without the other one seeing. They both knew the oath had no teeth.

They scoured the place, looking in every nook and cranny, in any non-obvious hiding place, trying their best to think like a crook. But nothing of value turned up, not a thing, because Mykola had beaten them to it. He had already snooped around, claiming his findings to cover this month's rent and damages, no remorse required.

Alpha had a large collection of Playboy magazines, a few favourite clothing items, and a lot of guns and knives. They took the guns and knives to the Police station. They gave the Playboy magazines to the old Greek at the corner store who would resell them to high school boys coming in for a Pepsi. They gave away his clothing to the Salvation Army who would make sure that others made good use of his unusual collection of fancy print Ascots and his pedantically sparkling white tank undershirts.

Mykola asked Antonio if he would come over to help clean the place to prepare for new tenants, to which Antonio readily agreed. He brought Isabella with him, and together with Olena, the four of them scrubbed and repainted, unclogged drains and disinfected the bathroom, and steamed grease off the kitchen cupboards and wall tiles. Marko and Peter helped by selling whatever was left behind in a kind of mini-market out front on the sidewalk. They had heard about the Playboys and had already lifted copies for themselves plus a few more to resell at a high price to their clueless friends. A successful scheme—their parents thought these boys had a future.

Antonio didn't think so though. He'd seen how little appreciation they seemed to show Olena for all the hard work she did for them and how little respect they seemed to show their father, and how they avoided contact with both of them so their parents wouldn't catch on to how rotten they were. Antonio kept his thoughts to himself but couldn't help comparing and noticing how different his relationship was with his own mother. He knew it was partly because of his nature, but partly because his mother gave no room to insolence and was quick to use a slipper or a wooden spoon as a threat. Olena's boys were spoiled and uncorrected, and cared for no one except themselves.

As dinnertime approached, Mykola stopped, took a deep breath, puffing out his cheeks as he blew out slowly. It had been a long couple of days with many tasks and he was satisfied with the results. They'd gotten a lot done and the place looked very presentable. With the new paint job covering over the smell of cigar smoke, and with the carpets and hallway runner removed, the smells of spilled, stale beer and rough-house whisky were gone as well.

They'd forgotten to move the fridge and stove away from the wall to face whatever grossness was found there, but Antonio volunteered to do that the next day, after a good night's rest. Olena thanked Antonio for offering and joked that he was taking this very seriously, as if he were preparing it for himself.

"I am, for me and Ma", he replied, more boldly than he intended. "If you'll have us back", he added.

Mykola and Olena laughed and almost cried with relief. Having tenants that they knew, liked, and trusted would be a real gift.

After Isabella and Antonio left, a tired Mykola and Olena climbed up the stairs to the third floor. They checked with the Americans to see if they were still comfortable living there after the unexpected murder of Alpha.

Clearly the young men had already discussed it among themselves because their spokesman offered, with the others nodding in agreement, that they were more comfortable now that Alpha was gone. The event had, strangely, made them feel homesick because problems requiring police intervention were commonplace where they were from.

Not to worry though, they wouldn't be phoning their parents about this. They didn't want to be pulled out of a place they had trusted to be dead simple safe. The less their parents knew, the better.

Trying Them On

As Mykola readied himself for a well-deserved sleep, Olena pulled out the pointe shoe bag from her front closet. Excitement trumped her tiredness and granted her a second wind.

"Mykola, I'm going back to the apartment upstairs for a few minutes. I forgot to do something," she told him vaguely.

After the emptying and the cleaning, their voices had echoed off the barren walls and the shiny, polished wooden floor of Alpha's old apartment. With no furniture in the rooms, it seemed so much bigger. In Olena's mind, the empty apartment had transformed completely into a studio of her very own and she wanted to take advantage before Isabella moved back in.

She sat on the living room floor and slipped on a shoe, wrapping and tying the ribbons as she'd learned from watching the girls. First one, then the other. With a little effort, she pushed herself back up again and moved over to the windowsill that was just about the perfect height to be her very own "pretend" barre. The room echoed with the funny sound of her elongated toeboxes slapping on the wood.

First through fifth position pliés, copying what she'd seen the girls do, Olena thought this was easy and she felt good and in control. "I feel so graceful", she thought.

But when she tried standing on her toes, she wobbled and winced in pain. This surprised her because the girls had always made it look so, well, natural. Of course, only weighing ninety pounds probably worked in their favour.

She tried to stand on pointe once more, but Madame Laflamme's words rang so true. It must, indeed, be best to start young, never mind even attempting a fouetté.

That was quite enough for her; dreaming was clearly easier. Deciding to just hang up the pointe shoes on her bedroom wall as a nice decoration, she untied the ribbons, whispered goodbye to her lifelong yearning, and shut down her studio for good.

Tenants Resettled

Isabella and Antonio hauled all their belongings back to the second floor apartment above Mykola and Olena. Two strong-backed shipping department workers from the factory made a little extra cash for helping with the move. They were motivated to give up their Saturday by fondness and respect for both Olena and Antonio, and the promise of a case of beer each.

The two workers had strong encouragement from the women at the factory. There had been rumours that Antonio and Olena were moving in together, so naturally, the curious women wanted the men to spy and report everything back to them. The anticipation of something juicy made the thought of returning to work on Monday more bearable.

Mykola helped to schlep the more delicate items, small boxes full of china and crystal, framed pictures, mirrors, and porcelain knick-knacks of all sorts and sizes. Olena helped Isabella to put things in their correct approximate location. Marko and Peter had, of course, made themselves scarce. Their excuse was that they were also helping friends move.

"Sounds good, boys. Don't hurt yourselves," remarked Mykola.

Out of earshot, Marko mocked, "Don't hurt yourselves moving all that nicked loot. And don't hurt yourselves by getting caught."

Marko and Peter laughed all the way. If their parents only knew.

Social Service

Olena's little idea to help her practise speaking English had worked very well. Now she spent far less time working out translations and her thoughts were often in English. These were the marks of someone who had crossed the language divide. She had also picked up a decent amount of French at work, surprising coworkers from time to time with what she knew. The more confidence she gained, the less inclined she was to continue her calling game.

It had been quite some time since Olena plucked random numbers out of her phonebook. She didn't even remember with whom she spoke the last time. However, she did remember the thrill of the hunt, of finding someone, anyone, who would speak with her for at least a few minutes.

With some rare spare time on her hands, Olena pulled out the heavy phonebook and gave it another try.

Riffling through the pages and throwing a dart-like finger at a number, she dialed it and waited as the phone rang its way up to fifteen. Her heart-rate quickened with a long forgotten anticipation. Will someone answer? Will they want to talk? Or will they just hang-up?

"Hello?" answered a low, mature male voice.

"Hello…I'm sorry…" Olena had picked up the Canadian knack of apologizing.

"I know it is strange, but would you mind speaking with me for a few minutes. I am trying to improve my English."

There was a pause.

Expecting to hear the familiar click of a hang-up, Olena was surprised to hear the man say, "Well, perhaps tomorrow. Could you call back tomorrow? I'm just on my way out the door."

Olena had never before been asked to call back. None of her random calls ever went beyond one connection. She quickly underlined the number with a pen and dog-eared the page so she could get back to it. Tomorrow.

At roughly the same time the next day, maybe a little later, Olena tried the number again. Fifteen rings and the man didn't answer. Was he out? Or was he ignoring her, thinking she was a nut?

She poured herself a coffee and sat at her green Formica kitchen table, debating whether she should try again. The kitchen door was open a crack to let in some fresh air. A cool breeze wafted through the door and whispered faintly under her naked feet. It had been a long time since she felt cool air between her toes, and she liked it.

Back at the small table in the dining room corner nook, she dialed the number again. And counted.

One…two…three… At thirteen rings, someone finally picked up.

"Hello?" said the same voice.

"Oh, yes, hello. Yesterday you asked me to call back," Olena said hesitantly, as a sort of introduction.

He said he remembered and he was glad she did. He explained that he had just returned from a short walk with his grandchildren, twin boys. His assignment was to bring them home from school and watch them until their father got home. He had to be extra careful crossing Boulevard St Joseph with them because the drivers were crazy and he was having trouble judging their speed these days. His eyes weren't as good as they used to be.

Without leaving an opening for Olena to jump in, he went on to say how he loved the boys and they made him laugh, but they exhausted him completely. He was an old man, some days unwilling or able to get out much, but the boys filled him with their energy and he managed well if he sat in the recliner while they ran loose around the apartment.

Olena listened as he talked and talked. She wasn't getting much practise at all, not a word in edgewise. Clearly, this man lacked adult company. He told her about his son, a civil engineer, who was hoping to work on the just-selected Expo 67 site. He told her about his daughter-in-law, now in Ottawa tending to her mother who had had a stroke. He spoke proudly about stepping in to help watch the boys while she was away.

And then he said, "Oh no, they're up to something dangerous. I have to go. Please call me here tomorrow."

He hung up softly. Click.

On top of not having said more than ten words during their call, Olena was now truly speechless. How had this man taken control of her hobby so easily? He had gotten her to call back, and now he was asking for more. He dominated the conversation and didn't ask about her at all. And then he hung up without saying goodbye to tend to something that was important only to him. She would not give him the satisfaction of calling back. Not tomorrow at least.

She let a whole day pass. When she got home from work, and before Mykola and the boys were home, she couldn't help herself. She dialed the number again.

"Hello?" he said.

"Hello, it's me again. Is this a good time?"

She wasn't ready to give him her name. Or to ask him for his. That would be too personal, too quickly.

"Now is good. The boys are breaking things but they're in their bedroom."

And then he started talking again. Olena was going to cut him off and interject, but didn't because he said, "I'm sorry. Last time I talked too much. I don't get many calls."

So maybe Olena was right. He could be just a lonely old man.

Then he added, "I'd like to ask you a question, if that's ok."

"Yes, of course. What is it?" asked Olena, eager to hear something that might allow her to speak.

A pause…and then…a heavy breath.

"What are you wearing?" the man said slowly.

Olena hung up with a slam. Click.

Chapter 5

Knock Knock 1963

Guilty Hold-Out

The old Serbian man, a bingo friend of Isabella's, turned the envelope over in his hands a few times to check its front and back for clues, and then pulled out the letter from inside. Teodor sat in a large wingback chair, swaddled in quilts to insulate himself from the cold in his apartment. Winter ice had caused a transformer to blow somewhere nearby and his block was left without power for hours.

Isabella waited for him to come to some sort of a conclusion. He used a magnifying glass now for reading with his one good eye, and his slightly shaking hand made it difficult to focus on the cursive, Cyrillic writing.

The letter had arrived in Isabella's mailbox instead of Mykola's, so she was convinced that she was entitled, indeed obliged, to open it. Being more than a little superstitious, she believed it must be a bad omen or it simply would have landed in the correct mailbox. She felt she had a duty to know what it was about so she could protect her friends from some unknown evil. If this turned out to be the wrong thing to do, well, she would have another thing to discuss with her priest in the confessional.

Teodor took a long time to read the letter even though it wasn't very long. Isabella sat wearing her coat, scarf, and gloves, and she could see her breath when she asked him what it said. There was a pause, and then Teodor admitted that the vocabulary was different from what he knew, but it seemed to say that a woman named Julianna loves a man named Mykola and she wishes to meet up with him soon. He should write back to her to let her know if he feels the same way.

Isabella was right. There was something untoward about this letter. Wasn't it lucky that it had fallen into her hands? If she got rid of it, Mykola wouldn't know that Julianna had tried to reach him. Julianna wouldn't receive a reply from Mykola. Olena wouldn't know anything about it and a marriage would be saved. And Isabella would earn extra points for negotiation with St. Peter when the time came. Isabella was always lightning-fast at coming up with a chain of plausible justifications.

Teodor was not very thrilled about being put in the position of aiding and abetting a mail theft. He didn't really like Isabella because she talked too much, meddled in people's business, and bragged too much each time she won a bingo game. So he held back the little detail that Julianna was coming to visit, whether Mykola replied or not. Isabella's interference would have no effect, the scenario would play itself out, and Isabella's victory would be Isabella's defeat. If he couldn't beat her at bingo, he could beat her at chess.

Telling Isabella

She could still hear it, the change in tone and intention. The beginning of something she wasn't ready for. Olena had to tell someone and, of course, that someone would be Isabella.

Isabella was aware of Olena's English practise routine but hearing about it before had never been so interesting. As Olena described the rather one-sided conversation with the man, she and Isabella got the giggles, and laughed and laughed, imagining how the rest of that wicked conversation could have gone.

"So, what's his name? Who is he?" asked Isabella.

Olena said she didn't ask and neither did he. It was like a mysterious rendezvous on a midnight train.

Isabella admitted that she had never had, nor thought of making, a call like that. She wanted to be the one who called him back. Give him a little thrill by having not one but two women call him and string him along for a while.

Olena dialed the number from Isabella's phone. They felt like school girls pranking someone. Olena waited to hear the man's voice to make sure it was him and not his son.

After the signature voice "Hello", she thrust the receiver into Isabella's hand, who did her best turn at sounding seductive. She talked for quite a few minutes, as only Isabella could, surprising Olena with what she knew from romance novels that she had read.

Standing beside Isabella with her ear as close to the phone as she could get, Olena could hear when the man began to talk. He was clearly playing along, his voice low and rumbling. Isabella's eyes suddenly widened and her mouth opened in a gasp. Olena mouthed "What? What did he say?" as Isabella exclaimed to him, "So sorry! Wrong number!" and quickly hung up.

Isabella began to laugh so hard, tracks of mascara ran down rivers of tears. Between gasps for air, she managed to say, "Oh, Olena! Out of all the numbers in your big, gigantic phonebook, you found the one for Teodor's son!"

A Quiet Day

It was a quiet day at the store. Rain was pelting down outside and streaking the shop windows. With fewer customers coming in, there was less water on the floor to mop up and more time for Mykola to think.

He couldn't get the image of the one-handed man out of his mind. It wasn't so much that particular person that had troubled him so much; that man seemed to be managing well with his predicament. For Mykola, it was the story told to him by Lubomir himself about what happened to his right hand so many years ago. Seeing the one-handed man in the store brought that old memory back all too vividly

Over time, Lubomir's version of Stefan's clear thinking and quick actions grew with hyperbole and sincere gratitude. Stefan was his hero and when he asked for a favour, to shelter Mykola, Lubomir was more than happy to do it.

Lubomir's Story, 1912

Lubomir and Stefan were two young friends in their late teens working together on a farm. They were sent to the blacksmith's workshop to pick up some newly forged horseshoes. As they entered, they noticed that the blacksmith wasn't there. His fire was burning and a rod was heating in the red-hot coals. Presumably he would be back soon to finish his task.

As they waited for him, they noticed a large number of metal augers on a low shelf, propped up in a standing pile against the wall. They had been sharpened and were waiting for the fence post diggers to come fetch them. Amongst the augers, there was a kind of log harpoon, seemingly put in the wrong place.

This pike pole attracted Lubomir's attention because it had an interesting metal hook at the end of a strong wooden shaft. He knew it was for controlling the logs that were being floated down the river and had nothing to do with making fence posts.

Thinking he would be helpful, Lubomir reached for the pike pole with the intention of putting it over to the side, but the bottom of the pole was jammed in on an angle behind the augers. He gave the stubborn pole a mighty tug and in a split second, hell broke loose.

The augers tumbled towards Lubomir with unstoppable inertia. They were heavy and numerous and sharp. Some of the handles hit Lubomir's head, causing him to stumble backwards, thankfully knocking himself out when his head hit the floor. Some of the blades landed on his forearm and if Stefan hadn't been there, Lubomir surely would have died.

As blood spurted from Lubomir's arm, Stefan knew he had to do something fast. He whipped off his belt and tied it tightly just past Lubomir's elbow. The blood stopped surging, but the augers had sliced through the muscle and cracked the bone, almost completely severing his forearm.

Stefan fought the gagging that he felt. He could smell the blood-iron on Lubomir's clothes and the stench of urine on his pants. There was no one there to help. He had to act fast and save his friend from bleeding out. He took out his pocket knife and cut off the rest of the connected tissue. He'd had some experience butchering pigs into hams, but now, here he was quite suddenly cutting up his friend. Later, he would recall that he didn't even really think. He just reacted and was finished in mere seconds.

It was hard to know if Lubomir was still unconscious from bumping his head, or from the shock and pain of the amputation. He didn't even flinch when Stefan took the rod from the fire and cauterized the wound. There was no concept of reattaching limbs, no guarantee of avoiding infection. This was as good as it was going to get.

Hearing this awful story from Lubomir, who got the embellished details from Stefan, Mykola wondered how he himself would have reacted in the same situation. He didn't really know if he could do it. Just thinking about it made him sick. It was odd how memories entwined with emotions where so hard to forget.

A Ring Instead of a Knock

November 11, 1963. Remembrance Day.

A hushing blanket of snow had already fallen overnight. Outdoor thermometers dipped down to near freezing and locked in for the winter. Those who ventured out to attend the service at the Montreal Cenotaph were hearty souls who knew how to survive with layers of wool and fur. With no work or school today, most people just stayed home, not braving the snowy roads nor bundling up their children against potential frostbite.

At precisely eleven o'clock in the morning, four military fly-over planes flew low in formation. Their slow, solemn droning, prolonged by overcast skies, spread a serious pall over all the free citizens below and sent a chill up the spines of Mykola and Olena. Only a few years prior in their homeland, that same sound drove them down into the cellar where they huddled and counted until the invaders' bombs stopped exploding, thankfully far enough away each time.

After dinner, Mykola was busy building a shelf in the boys' back bedroom when he heard their new installed-by-Antonio doorbell ring. Olena, in the living room close to the front of the apartment, moved quickly to the double-doored vestibule, closing the inner door behind her and flicking on the porch light. Peering through the outer door's glass pane, she saw a young woman whose smooth-skinned, pink-cheeked face was encircled by a furry hat. An iconic Hudson's Bay multi-striped wool scarf was tied stylishly around her neck.

Olena opened the outer door and begged the sweet, young Canadian woman to step inside so they could talk without freezing. From a hand-made backpack that was slung over her shoulder, the woman pulled out a sheet of paper from which she would read the transliteration of a very important message. Pausing to take a breath and settle her nerves, the young woman surprised Olena when she began to speak in a strong and familiar accent.

"I am Julianna. My mother, Danusia, has died and I am here to find Mykola. He is my father," she read.

Of course, Olena was taken completely by surprise.

"What?! What are you talking about?" she sputtered.

Julianna had hoped for a more welcoming response, but she expected her arrival to cause some stress. She explained further, keeping difficult news simple.

"My mother and Mykola were married when they were very young. I swear on my mother's grave. This is the absolute truth," replied Julianna.

"Noh, I don't think so. I would have known this," Olena replied. "This cannot be true. Who *are* you, really?"

Mykola was curious about what was going on. It was strange to have an unexpected visitor at that time of night. The women's voices were muffled by the closed inner door, but Olena's words seemed sharp. Maybe she needed his help, he wondered. He moved through the small kitchen into the dining room. As he approached the front door to get a better look, he heard the woman ask, "May I please see Mykola? He will tell you."

Olena re-opened the inner door and stepped back into the apartment. With a sinking feeling in his stomach, Mykola recognized that scowl on her face. It meant he was in big trouble.

In the narrow entryway, Olena pressed up against the wall to make room for the unexpected visitor who came around from behind her. Seeing her face, Mykola stood dismayed. Was this Danusia? The young woman looked so much like her, but Danusia just couldn't be that young anymore.

His eyes were drawn to the woman's scarf, the scarf that he himself had sent only a few months ago. The oddest sensation ran over the top of his brain, feeling and sounding like tiny beads being poured out of a flask, some kind of a shock response that lasted only a few seconds.

He realized who she was.

No one moved.

The young woman, with hazel eyes not unlike Mykola's, was staring at him, and his eyes darted from her to Olena. His flight instinct kicked in and he just wanted to bolt to his grandfather's house as he often did when he was a little boy in trouble. But Olena was blocking the door, hands on hips, and in any case, his grandfather was long gone. Half a world plus six feet away.

"Mykola?" asked Julianna, although she already knew. Adrenaline caused her voice and her knees to shake. She tried her best not to show how nervous she felt. She was very smart to wear the scarf; it was a clear and simple confirmation of her identity. For her most recent birthday, Mykola had sent it to her, a lucky luxury find in the window of a second-hand shop while he was on a delivery run on the other side of town.

Mykola stood with his mouth fish-flapping; no words coming out. Just as it was becoming clear to Olena that he had kept an old secret from her, their sons Marko and Peter came tumbling in from outside. They were rarely at home anymore, always out with their friends and returning for food, sleep, and quick hello-goodbye hugs with their mother and, sometimes, their father.

The boys still carried the scent of cigarette smoke and alcohol from the pool hall in Chinatown where they regularly sharked their way to a decent amount of money. They had been forbidden from returning there after being rounded up in a police raid a few months ago. Facing real parental anger and embarrassment for the first time in public at the police station wasn't something the boys ever wanted to do again, but the lure of the vice and easy money was too strong. The smell was an obvious clue for Mykola and Olena to know exactly where they had been.

Luckily, tonight, their timing was perfect. They had stumbled into a strange, silent hornet's nest and their transgression was, at least temporarily, ignored. They stared at the beautiful stranger standing in the warm entryway, still all bundled up in her winter clothing. The growing crowd forced Julianna to back up, bumping into the wall jutting out behind her. She felt a little claustrophobic as the boys and their smell filled what little space was left. Nevertheless, she found the words she had practiced over and over.

"Surprise boys, I am your sister."

Spill It

Olena told the wide-eyed boys to take Julianna to the kitchen to give her something to eat and something hot to drink. They could manage to make some food by themselves for a change. With this stranger's arrival, she'd been hit with a wave of disbelief. She motioned to Mykola, pointing to the living room so they could talk in private.

As he lowered himself onto the sofa, Mykola felt queasy. He sat leaning forward, elbow on knee, hand on forehead, as he gathered his thoughts. After a few eternal, uncomfortable minutes during which Olena said not a word, he braced both hands on his knees and took a deep breath, eyes on the floor.

He sensed her laser glare boring a hole through his brain just for kicks.

His story began slowly, first like thick syrup, then speeding up like running water. He told the whole truth as he remembered it, feeling the life-long burden lifting off his broken-mended heart. Layered in the context of teenage encounters, he described to Olena the timeframe, the crazy mushrooms that he and Danusia ate, and his parents' acceptance of the pregnancy. But Danusia's parents' later interference, the separation plan, and the shame cast on him by the old village hags had forced him to run and hide his truth forever.

Mykola swept his history out from its hiding place under the rug, its dusty cloud now hanging in the air in front of Olena for exactly the first time.

He had never spoken to her about his involvement with Danusia and the birth of their daughter Julianna, or the circumstances by which they became estranged. Only once, he had confided in his cousin Gregory and, because of Olena's surprised reaction, he knew that Gregory had taken his secret to the grave.

Mykola had never expected Julianna to appear at his home. He had always put his address on the envelopes of the cards he sent for her birthday, feeling she had a right to know where he lived. But he never, ever thought it would really happen given the distance, time, and money it would take to pull it off. He certainly would have appreciated some warning of her arrival so that he could have smoothed the way instead of being blind-sided. It was all too embarrassing and abrupt.

Olena took it all in, breathing deeply to stay calm, listening carefully as Mykola unraveled his story. She found herself feeling somewhat sympathetic towards the very young people who made a mistake. But suddenly, she snapped right out of it. This wasn't some over-and-done fable about strangers in a far-away land. It was an on-going secret saga that involved her very own husband, whom she thought she knew.

A Knock Instead of a Ring

It was all too much for her. She needed to think and she didn't want to hear any more from Mykola. Olena took off out the front door and up the steep, snow-covered Montreal staircase to Isabella's apartment right above. Out of habit and having forgotten about the new doorbells, Olena knocked urgently on Isabella's front door, but she wasn't home. Instead, her handsome son Antonio opened the door and let Olena in.

Antonio was surprised to see Olena so upset. She wasn't even wearing a coat on this very cold night. He pulled a Hudson's Bay blanket that had been warming along the top of the living room radiator and wrapped Olena in it to warm her up. She bristled a little at the coincidence of seeing multi-stripes twice in one night.

As he pulled the edges together tightly across her chest, he found himself a little too close to his "tesoro mio". He was about to pull out a second yellow card on himself when she leaned in and gave him a sweet, soft, lingering kiss on the lips. He didn't move except for his eyebrows shooting skyward, and he only asked, "What is wrong?"

Olena explained, with few details, that Mykola had betrayed her and now that she had betrayed him also, they might be considered a little closer to even.

Antonio didn't really care what the reason was. He didn't care that she was using him in this moment. He didn't hang any hope on his quiet love turning into something bigger. However, he took a little advantage of his own and held her tight until she relaxed and brushed his cheek with another kiss.

"We can't, you know," sighed Antonio.

Olena stepped away and unwrapped herself, saying, "I know. I'm very sorry to bother you with all this. I have to get back."

Then in a flash, only hesitating briefly to steel herself at her own front door, she was back downstairs sitting tensely along with everyone else at the dining room table, a safe distance from the kitchen knives.

They didn't hear the piece of floorboard being removed above their heads. Antonio had discovered the loose board when they renovated the apartment after Alpha's demise. Taking out the board and laying flat on the floor with his ear towards it, he could hear their conversations below or at least get the gist of them. He never did this when Isabella was home, and he never knew that she did it too when he wasn't there. Sometimes their curiosity became their entertainment. Sometimes it became their burden.

We're Back

Mykola had managed to squelch the hideous sound of the old village hags from his mind for years.

The whole town knows what you did, Mykola.

Be ashamed forever. This is the curse we have put upon you.

Now those words awoke. They stretched their muscles after their long sleep and snaked around Mykola's ankles, flipping him sharply upside down.

Coming Clean

He was living a decent and respectable life, and proving the hags wrong in their indictment of irresponsibility. But now his secret had been abruptly laid wide open and he felt equal parts ashamed for lying to Olena, happy to see his daughter at last, and at a total loss for how to proceed.

It was Olena's express desire to make this problem go away as soon as possible. She fought her innate reflex to throw Julianna out into the street for disturbing their lives without warning. But she needed to give her a chance to explain why she had come and what she expected. Otherwise, they might never know her motivation for coming. Or worse yet, she might have a motivation for staying!

So Olena let Julianna talk. She spoke using a mixture of mostly English and their common native language, fluidly intertwining both when a word or an expression gap occurred. Julianna had put many hours into practising and studying to be ready for coming to Canada some day, and as a result, her English vocabulary and grammar were tentative but quite understandable.

The boys sat transfixed by her. They had to remind themselves that this stranger was their sister. Now that she had dropped into their lives, they wanted to hear the whole story.

Julianna explained that the transliteration on her paper note was just in case she needed to bolster her confidence when the door first opened, since she had no idea what to expect.

To put Olena and Mykola more at ease, Julianna declared that she didn't intend to stay long. Upon finally meeting her father in person, she could be at peace now and her mother's spirit would be satisfied. She described her arduous voyage by train, then boat, and then train again. It was far from easy, but she felt it was worth it. She didn't want anything from Mykola besides perhaps a bit of time to get to know him. She knew what traits she had in common with her mother and she was curious to see what came from her father.

Julianna described how she and her mother had lived with her grandparents, how her mother had married and widowed and never married again, and how she had died from pneumonia a few months ago. There was a severe lack of available medicine, and their local doctor was overworked and inexperienced, and was really not much help at all. And now, Julianna was quite alone in this world.

On her deathbed, Danusia implored Julianna to make the journey to Montreal to see the man, her father, who had never forgotten her. Allowing a little pent-up angst to leak out, Olena slapped her hand on the table and asked Julianna how she knew he'd never forgotten.

Julianna was ready with proof. She glanced at Mykola and reached into her backpack.

The boys side-glanced each other and held their breath. Mykola felt a large glob of sweat roll down his back, moistening the waistband of his pants. Out came a packet of envelopes, twenty-seven in all, each containing a card that he'd sent. In the bottom right-hand corner, hand-written after delivery, was the amount of money they'd found inside. As Julianna placed the packet in front of Olena and locked eyes with Mykola, she said quietly, "It is Remembrance Day in more ways than you expected."

No Sleep

During the ride to work with Antonio the next morning, Olena had a raging headache from lack of sleep. Mykola had been unusually agitated, tossing and turning, and had shouted "Witches!" a few times during the night. He quieted down eventually and just as Olena's brain felt a wash of melatonin, he started up again, pulling the blanket, tossing and shouting some more. Even though she wasn't getting any sleep at all, she felt some satisfaction that his sleep was tortured, like being chased by devils with long, sharp tridents poking his muscles and making him suffer, doing the dirty work for her.

Antonio had heard enough through the floor. He didn't have to ask any questions.

In the evening, Olena went upstairs to see Isabella. She needed to vent with a friend to sort out her thoughts. Isabella already knew some things from Antonio, but she listened carefully, not really knowing what advice to give for a change.

After mulling over the situation, Isabella couldn't help herself. She came downstairs with Olena and suggested sincerely to Mykola that he should spend some time with Julianna before she was gone forever. He would regret it if he didn't.

Olena stood by, stone-cold, allowing Isabella to run the show on her behalf. Mykola tried not to look at his wife. This was not the time to provoke a reaction accidentally.

Antonio offered him directions to Julianna's rooming house, which puzzled Mykola. How did Antonio know where she was staying? Instead of getting into it, he thanked him, and walked over to Olena's phone to call his boss to take the next day off work.

Olena scowled and huffed, and Isabella took that as her cue to leave. Mykola had never taken an impromptu day off for Olena, and although she knew this was an unusual situation, it would be yet another point of contention.

At the Door

Julianna wasn't expecting Mykola when he knocked on her door at around noon. Without knowing how else to start, he asked her if she was hungry. She smiled, said yes, and felt a slight pang at the fatherly question. They decided to go to the Jazz Bar down the block that Mykola had noticed when he walked by. It was a popular nighttime joint, but was much quieter and less crowded around lunchtime. They sat at a table near the north-facing window, its café-style curtains blocking the bright light that reflected off the sparkling snow outside.

The waitress brought their food and drinks, and then observed them from afar while she folded napkins and prepped the bar for the evening rush. Her favourite thing to do was to watch people and try to figure out their backstory. She was hardly ever correct, but her imagination winged her away from her boring, routine job. She noticed that the nervousness of these two people subsided quickly, and that he looked old enough to be the woman's father. Sure, some men just liked younger women. He was probably married, she guessed. She'd seen it many times before.

It was awkward at first, but as the minutes passed, Mykola and Julianna took turns, and became more relaxed and comfortable talking about themselves and getting to know each other.

Julianna noticed that they were both left-handed, although Mykola ate holding his fork with his right hand. She noticed that he squinted when looking into the distance, as did she from near-sightedness. Their eye colour was nearly the same, an uncommon hazel greenish-brown, and their hair colour was a similar light-brown shade that bleached easily in the sun.

These were small details that bound them together as proof of paternity, but other similarities ran a little deeper. They were both patient, generally kind, and pragmatic. They were both excellent at arithmetic, and they both disliked the smell of fish, diesel exhaust, and wet dogs with a passion.

Mykola explained to Julianna why he hadn't been a bigger part of her life, and that he regretted it, but he was so glad that she had grown up brave and independent. She replied, a little ruefully, that she hadn't really had a choice, but she wasn't bitter. She had a happy childhood, and she was extremely grateful for the cards he sent. She looked forward to them every year and they arrived without fail. Growing up, her best friend had a father who ignored her right in the very same house, so Julianna appreciated that she had a thoughtful father who did what he could, even from far away.

They came into the Jazz Bar as remote father and distant daughter. After the four hours they spent together, until the owner eventually asked them to leave before the dinner crowd began arriving, they left as friends.

She took his hand and gave it a squeeze, reminding him that she would be leaving soon, back to her home. She told him that spending even just this short time with him was the best thing that ever happened to her, and maybe someday she would come again. Mykola was certainly welcome to visit her as well. He laughed, asking if she thought his old village was safe. She understood and replied that probably no one had filled the witches' pointy boots, yet, and there was no one like that in her town either, thank goodness.

Julianna would be travelling back across the ocean on a third-class ticket. She bought the cheapest ticket both ways, knowing that some women got to eat at the Captain's table, but she had set her sights on sleeping in the Captain's bed.

Unfinished Business

Three days after Julianna's surprise visit, there was a note for Olena on the kitchen table when she returned from work. The boys had taken their father to the pool hall so he could have a drink and play a game or two.

At first, Olena was angry that they went where they were forbidden. Then she was annoyed at not being included. She needed a break too, a little time for frivolous fun, but the boys hadn't thought about her, as usual. At least today had been a good day at work for a change, with little Mighty Maria bringing in a Portuguese cake to share for her birthday, and with nothing breaking and no deadlines missed.

At home alone, it was much too quiet. Olena was restless; she felt like there was something she needed to do. She could go to the pool hall and join them, but she really didn't want to fill her lungs with someone else's cigarette smoke more than she already did at work. Anyway, she hoped that

Mykola was being punished further by being sharked by his own flesh and blood.

Olena let her thoughts percolate as she ate a quick supper of leftover beef stew and salad. What bubbled up was that she still had unfinished business with Julianna. Olena had to make sure Julianna wasn't doing some sharking of her own. After putting away her supper dishes and a few items she bought at the Greek's store, and opening the mail that had been delivered that day, she decided to take the bus to the rooming house where Julianna was staying while in town.

Rooming House

After hunting up and down the street on slippery sidewalks, Olena finally found the address she was looking for. The enameled plates of white numbers on cobalt blue were quite pretty up-close but were hard to see from the street. It was an unwelcome sign of aging that Olena's eyes weren't as sharp as they once were. Luckily her job didn't involve threading the sewing machine needles any more.

She carefully picked her way up the steep, narrow Montreal staircase that was glistening with frost, holding onto the glossy, black pipe railing that was a little too low, another ignored building code infraction. Reaching the second floor porch-like landing, she was very glad that she and Mykola had chosen their first floor apartment when they moved in. They hadn't really given a thought to how winter might affect those stairs, exposed to the elements as they were.

She knocked on the door several times. No lights were on and there was no answer. Olena peered over the railing of the landing into the shimmering street below. All of the trees that lined the street had lost their leaves, but their thickets of branches made it hard to see the entire length of the block. Directly in front of the apartment, she observed a young couple hustling by with a well-wrapped baby in a pram, an older gentleman walking his dog and pretending not to notice the snow yellowing at the edge of the sidewalk, and a car driving slowly down the one-way street trolling for a parking spot, its tailpipe blowing clouds behind it.

It was much too cold to wait around outside in the freezing weather. The sky was completely clear and black with very few stars showing in the city lights, and no cloud-blanket to hold in the city warmth.

Olena was disappointed that she couldn't settle things with Julianna just yet. She lingered a bit longer, dreading the chute-like descent of the stairs to the sidewalk, but after making it down safely and walking down the street back to the bus stop, the small neon sign of the Jazz Bar beckoned her with a faint flicker.

From the doorstep, she heard the lilting of a saxophone played with much more profession than the boy next door, and she decided that a short drink and some good music would lighten her sour mood.

Jazz Bar

Stepping inside, her eyes adjusting to the dimness, Olena was surprised to spy Antonio sitting at a small table in the darkened room. His back was against the wall so he saw her too when she came inside. He motioned for her to come over.

There were two drinks on the table and a second chair that was pushed back, with a coat hanging over it. As Olena approached, she noticed a scarf that had fallen to the floor, the scarf with the stripes. What was going on here? Where is she?

Antonio stood up and got another chair, but Olena put up her hand in the signal for "Stop". Speaking loudly to be heard over the music, she asked him incredulously, "Why are you here with Julianna?"

Of course, the song that the band was playing ended just as she said, "... here with Julianna?" so loudly that a few patrons looked away from the band and turned to stare at her. After they stopped glaring, Antonio answered, "She is leaving tonight."

Already returning to the table, Julianna watched the brief confrontation from the corridor leading to the toilets in the back. She had hoped to make a quick, early exit to the train station, but now Olena had spoiled her own surprise.

Julianna felt quite alarmed that Olena was there. She felt a flush on her neck and cheeks, and goosebumps tingled down her arms. Why was Olena following her?

She had already figured out that Antonio was a man of few words. Privately in her own head, she joked that maybe, just maybe, she knew more English than he did. She knew she would have to do the talking to explain what was going on. She closed her eyes and held back for a minute to conjure up the words she needed, finding it hard to explain or defend herself in a language different from her own so that Antonio could understand her and back her up.

Train Tonight

Getting back to the table and picking up her scarf, she said as warmly as she could, "Hello Olena. I'm glad you came."

She leaned in for an air-hug with Olena who stood her ground, and then the three of them sat at the table waiting for the band to take a break. It was an uncomfortable ten minutes or so, until the music stopped.

Not knowing how long the break would be, Julianna began explaining right away that on the night she first visited, Antonio had offered to go with her to her rooming house to ensure she arrived safely. She didn't know how he knew that she was visiting Olena and Mykola, or when she would be leaving, but he called down to her from his front porch and for some reason, she trusted his face.

Antonio knew because he had listened through the gap in the floor until he heard Isabella's key in the front door's lock.

Tonight he escorted her to the nearby train station, but the train she had booked to Halifax was running late because of the icy weather. Instead she would leave later tonight if the train arrived, or maybe tomorrow if it was still held up. Since she had spent some time with Mykola, short as it was, she felt good and there was no reason to stay and disrupt lives any further.

Julianna and Antonio were simply killing time in a warm bar instead of in a cold, cavernous station where the seats had been taken out to discourage the homeless from taking refuge there. She had hoped that her arrival at their home would have gone smoother and friendlier because of the letter she had written and sent well in advance.

Crossed Signals

Up to that last statement, Olena listened carefully and asked very few questions. She understood and accepted the explanation about tonight, and her small amount of jealousy at seeing Antonio and Julianna together dissipated.

But.

"What letter are you talking about?" questioned Olena.

Julianna looked surprised. She had sent a letter three months ago so it would have time to arrive before she did.

"You didn't receive it? Oh, you didn't *know* I was coming."

She now understood the confusion at the door when she arrived, and why Mykola might have been in so much trouble.

Julianna explained that she had sent a letter written in her own hand. Perhaps the postman couldn't decipher it? Maybe it got lost, or maybe it would still come but it would be too late. She did not know what happened to it. It was a short note to tell Mykola that she would like to meet him and that he should reply if he wanted to, but she would come regardless if he answered or not. She needed to settle her mother's spirit.

Antonio said not a word. Several weeks ago, when he shook out Isabella's bedroom garbage can into the larger bin in the alley, a light blue Airmail envelope floated out of it and settled on the ground at his feet. He wondered why an opened envelope addressed to Mykola would be in her garbage can. He picked it up and examined the strange, unfamiliar script. He pulled out the letter partway, but not being able to read what it said, he chucked it into the bin, went on to do other chores, and forgot all about it.

As it neared the time that the late train was expected, Antonio stood up from the table and motioned to Julianna that it was time to go. She got up, did up her coat, and wrapped the scarf around her neck, tucking the striped ends between her top two buttonholes.

Olena remained seated, finishing the drink she had ordered, a stiff one, and then felt a rush to get up and give Julianna a real hug. Although she still had big things to resolve with Mykola, in particular the money he had sent, she actually found it in her heart to feel sorry for Julianna who had never really had a father and now she had no mother, and she had taken a big risk coming here on her own.

A brave girl, like one jumping off a big swing into a large pile of unknown. She had no way of knowing whether the pile would offer a soft landing or a prongs-up pitchfork. She ended up with a bit of both.

Sharks

Having lost all the money in his wallet to his sons, Mykola was finally beginning to realize that they had needed more supervision and a stronger hand to guide them as they were growing up. He and Olena had put their energies towards resettling, paying their debts, and in Mykola's case, working a few schemes of his own to make some extra, undocumented cash. The two boys worked their schemes out on their own, sometimes successfully, mostly not.

There had been letters of reprimand from their teachers and a few bail-outs from jail, but they had better sense than to ever bring their friends over to their home. They understood that their shady friends' language and shifty eyes would have made Olena and Mykola feel very uncomfortable. The boys ran with an exciting but dangerous crowd, whose eyes would have cased the rooms and whose hands would have robbed the drawers. By never meeting their friends, Mykola and Olena were spared the kind of trouble doled out to many others and they never realized that their angels were falling.

Having spent too long in the pool hall that night, Mykola had allowed himself to get deeply inebriated, something he rarely did and so it was something for which he had little tolerance. In his younger days, drinking 'shine was a rite of passage and manhood, but it always made him feel sick, gave him a cracking headache, and made him worry that he would go blind. In his older years, he generally avoided alcohol and never smoked tobacco, to save money. But tonight he had to shake off the terribly disturbing nightmares he'd had, and steel himself against what was yet to come from Olena.

It was quite late already when Mykola decided to leave but the boys weren't finished yet, and having had too much to drink themselves, they didn't give a second thought to their father's state. Mykola took longer to put on his coat, having missed his sleeve several times. He padded his pocket to check for his now-empty wallet and he dipped unsuccessfully to find the house keys that were actually deep in his pants' pocket. No matter. Olena would let him in. Or would she? He almost hoped she wouldn't. He could wander all night or catch a nap with the mouse-catcher in the back room of one of his stores. Or just freeze to death on a park bench as fair punishment for his lying, secretive ways.

With all those thoughts and alcohol swirling in his brain, Mykola was in a deep state of distracted walking. He had turned in the wrong direction and was actually heading further away instead of closer to home. To cut the wind from freezing his ears, he flipped up the collar of his light-grey wool coat and lowered his chin, his eyes trying to focus on the icy walkway that made his unsteady gait even more so.

No one needed to pour extra alcohol on Mykola tonight; it was obvious that he was totally wasted. But still, why he didn't register the loud rumbling of the nighttime delivery truck hurtling through its right-of-way green light before he stepped out into the road, no one would ever know.

Morning Mourning

Around three o'clock in the morning, the good-for-nothing boys stumbled into the apartment, crawled into their beds like the bugs that they were, and fell fast asleep. Olena awoke at five-thirty to get ready for work, but Mykola's side of the bed was still made up. She checked the living room sofa, but he wasn't there either. This was the first time ever that he hadn't come home, and she was glad because she didn't want to talk to him yet. He'd be home for dinner for sure.

She wasn't finished processing everything that had happened in such a short time and she had an important staff meeting to deal with at work that day, for which she was not ready at all. She should have called in sick, but before she knew it, autopilot took over and she was ready to go when Antonio knocked on the door.

Except this time it wasn't Antonio.

Two police officers delivered the news that Mykola had been hit by a truck and had died sometime during the night. There were no witnesses, but the truck driver had stopped and frantically called the police from a nearby pay phone. Through his distress, he cooperated fully and was able to describe exactly what happened in a manner that gave the officers no reason to disbelieve.

Unintended

Teodor heard about an accident on the morning radio news report. The name of the victim had not been released, and the announcer moved on quickly to other items.

As Teodor was watering his huge Dieffenbachia plant by the front window, his pride and joy, he heard the sound of angry, short-step heels clacking on the icy sidewalk. Isabella was coming down the street and up to see him. She was putting out a lot of effort to get to him quickly, stepping into icy footprints, trying to keep her balance.

He winced. She was obviously very angry about something. It must have something to do with the letter, he surmised.

Isabella barged in and jabbed a skinny finger into his shoulder, screaming something in Italian. Teodor didn't need to understand the words to know it was something that would keep her in the confessional a little longer. She was so upset about Mykola's senseless death, she was angry that Teodor hadn't revealed Julianna's no-matter-what visit, but most of all, she needed to ensure that he would keep quiet about the letter.

Teodor assured her that he had nothing to gain by telling anyone about it; this was her problem to deal with and she should keep his name out of it or he would have no choice but to throw her under the bus. As far as the others knew, the letter never arrived and, as such, the events transpired regardless.

As Isabella was heading for the door, Teodor lobbed a parting shot. He hadn't appreciated her yelling at him. His voice went low and slow.

"Don't worry. I'm good at keeping secrets," he said. "I know who that was on the phone. Maybe you'll be nicer when you come back next time."

Isabella stopped abruptly, turned on her heel, and pointed at Teodor again, shooting him dead with her eyes. He shrank back a little, not knowing what was coming next.

"Do not EVER say that again or I will slap your face so hard! Just because her husband's dead now, don't think you can have phone sex with Olena. Or me. Forget about it!"

Chapter 6

Real Life

1963–1980

Growing Up Fast

It took the worst to make something good happen. Olena's boys were pulled up sharply by the hair by fate, slapped in the face by reality, and sobered up quickly by responsibility in the days after their father's funeral. It was a stunning turn of personality and habit, a monumental change of direction and conscious concern for others instead of only themselves, born from a truth—their father was dead, in very large part because of them and their disregard for anyone outside of themselves.

Probably for the first time, the boys saw their mother. Actually saw her. Recognized her as a person, vulnerable and heartbroken. She was trying to come to terms with Mykola's death and she spoke out loud to him a lot, settling old and recent grievances. For a while she had a lot to say, until she was all talked out. When she grew quieter, the boys couldn't tell what she was thinking. They worried about her and decided to do what they could to help.

Marko took on the funeral arrangements with Olena, including managing the wake and the mourners. He got into a scuffle with Stanley, the funeral home director, who pretended to be very solemn and respectful, all the while trying to upsell them on everything from casket to headstone. Imagine the scene of a scammer scamming a scammer!

Marko saw right through it and was having none of it. He negotiated the prices down to the bone after threatening to go public. But for about a week or so, after seeing how this essential business worked and realizing the fantastic profit margins, Marko seriously considered getting into the funeral business himself. However, this required special schooling, licensing, empathy, and not being creeped out by corpses, all of which quickly conspired to change his mind.

Peter had more trouble finding a role for himself at first but ended up taking on all of the financial tasks for Olena, such as the tax return and the probate. He was the one who handled all the illicit money in the boys' recent past. He was the one who thought he naturally fit the financial management role now. He was the one who could do figures quickly in his head, just like his father.

A few months after Mykola's funeral, with Peter feeling his ties strengthened with Olena as they actually spent time together wading through the details and procedures of the after-death together, Marko felt left out and under-utilized.

He was waking up at night in a cold sweat with his heart pounding from bad dreams he couldn't remember. He was losing money at the pool tables, getting marked as a man who had lost his touch. He was hearing his father whisper in his ear, turning to find that he was not there at all.

He felt miserable, useless, and aimless. And guilty. And ashamed. It was a lot to shoulder all at once, especially the guilt and the shame, emotions Marko had never felt. For all the stupid things he'd done in his life, he had never taken the outcomes so personally before, usually just laughing them off and moving on. This situation was completely different, closer, and his deeply buried innate reactions bubbled up to the surface and surprised him.

Peter noticed that Marko had withdrawn, but he was busy with the paperwork and was dealing with his own remorse and grief in his own way. Marko wasn't asking for help so Peter just left him alone; he would just have to get a grip and figure himself out.

Olena also noticed that Marko had withdrawn, but she wanted to give him some time and space to centre himself and reorient his life. She hoped that he would sprout a compass and grow in the direction of a good and productive life. Get a job. Buy a home. Get married. It was a simple formula but not the right formula for Marko.

The Bridge

He didn't remember how he had gotten there, but Marko steadied himself by the midspan railing of the mighty Jacques Cartier Bridge. It was ridiculous for him to be there, in the bitter, whipping cold night air but, in truth, he barely felt it having had too much to drink.

Mesmerized by the night view of the lights of the cityscape, he thought about how those lights symbolized success. Success in business, success in career. Bright, tall buildings that shone with pride in the night sky. A place where he would never work, never be, never fit. A place so different from the squat, humble three-storey buildings that made up his universe. Sturdy rowhouses that insisted they were just good enough, just what was needed to survive.

He looked down at the iced-over river far below, feeling a little swirl of vertigo and experiencing that strange tug that made him feel like jumping. He held on tighter and grappled with his thoughts in alcoholic slow-motion, wishing that Mykola could be there beside him.

What if he hit the ice and snapped his neck? Would that be quicker than drowning in the thawed flowing water of spring? How *does* one die from a snapped neck? Does it happen instantly? Does drowning hurt? What if he snapped his neck, cracked the ice, and then had to drown too? Both.

As he dared himself to think about how any of that would actually feel, a car full of high school boys drove by slowly, windows open, taunting him.

"Jump!"

"Fuck no!" shouted Marko, snapping out of his dark thoughts. He turned to run after the car full of little shits as they gunned it and sped off over the crest of the bridge and down to the bend in the road on Île Sainte-Hélène, out of sight. Their mocking laughter rang in Marko's ears, as he bent over to catch his breath, his windpipe burning from the cold air he'd sucked in running. He thought he heard them shout, "Loser!" too, but he wasn't sure.

The idiots in the car would never know that their thoughtless command to jump, barked out to harm Marko, had actually saved him. As a Taurus, he hated people telling him what to do, and, invariably, he would do the exact opposite.

Marko turned to walk back towards the city over the bridge that did not claim him. It was a long walk back, a long time to think while his head was clearing from its vodka fog. He decided that it was time to make a clean break, away from the lure of trouble-making. Away from everything that had been painted grey after Mykola's death. Away from the reminders that on the night he died, Mykola had needed Marko and Peter's help for the first and last time in his life.

Planting New Roots

There were "Jobs Out West", Marko read in the Gazette. Tree planting jobs where, if he worked fast and hard and long, he could make some good money. Tree planters worked outdoors and were part of a crew but were independent in how they wanted to carry out their tasks. The article included a picture of a glorious mountain top vista, with some smiling tree planters and an organized campsite in the background. This was for him, Marko thought. A complete change of scenery, away from trouble. This would be good for him.

Olena was happy that he'd finally made a decision. He had sprouted the compass she had wished for, but its directional needle pointed a lot further away than she had expected. When he first told her that he was going "West", she assumed the West Island of Montreal. There were several multi-national drug companies out there and many new housing developments. That would be a good place to start.

But instead, for the first time in his life, he set off on a train heading West across the country to join a tree planting crew of people from many parts of the world. Unlike his father, he hadn't researched the trip very well and he hadn't asked any people for advice beforehand, so it took him days longer to find the exact location because the West was a lot larger than he'd bargained for.

When Marko finally arrived at a crew meeting point, he soon realized that he was woefully unprepared for working in these conditions. He was a city boy, used to warm and dry, used to smooth roads and comfortable beds, used to his mother doing all the heavy lifting. Now, after all the pain of getting here, he found himself turned away by the crew chief who could recognize an arriving urban disaster from a mile away.

Marko felt ashamed at his failure to get things right. He retreated to the nearest town where he found a small group of young people, men and women, their backpacks with sleeping bags and shovels laid in a tidy heap beside them. They were gathered at a table on the sidewalk in front of the town bar, having lunch out in the sun and talking excitedly about returning to the planting camp to start their season.

Marko asked if they would help him. He needed to know what to buy, what life was like up there, and how much money he could make. As they filled him in, he learned that his up-front equipment costs would be quite high and he'd have to pay for food and lodging, he would only get paid a nickel per tree, and he would have to carry up to four hundred trees a day! Then they started bragging amongst each other about who planted the most last year and the numbers seemed staggering to Marko.

This wasn't easy work. This wasn't an easy location, not even to mention the blood-sucking black flies. There was no time or tolerance for complaints. You just had to shovel-and-shove all day long.

The group advised him to really think about what he was getting into before committing. They had already sussed him up and figured he would stand no chance. Taking one look at his soft city hands, they knew he would blister-up in the first five minutes and burst into tears.

Retreating

Inside the town bar, sitting near the beer spigots having himself a cold, crisp lager, Marko thought about everything he'd heard and his gut told him to run. He was in way over his head and he hadn't even started yet.

A short distance away in a second room towards the back of the building, he heard the all-too-familiar crack of a break.

No, no, no. Don't go.

He braced himself and tried to focus on the beer. It was a good one, made from mountain-fresh water that seemed to make a real difference. More sounds of a cue ball striking and the sweet sound of a sinking. It didn't take long before he gave in and wandered over to the other room, where six beautiful but well-worn tables awaited his prowess. And there he was, instantly back behind the eight ball again.

No Allies in the Alley

Something dripped on his face. Marko woke up to the snout of a large dog drooling over him, a smelly alley rat-dog that prowled the streets all night looking for restaurant scraps. His head hurt and when he tried to get up, he realized he'd been tossed onto an overflow of garbage beside a big, rusty dumpster. Blood from the gash on his forehead had trickled down to where he could taste it. He pulled himself together and wondered where his stuff was; hopefully still in the bar where he'd put it down sometime before his lights went out.

The woman behind the bar watched Marko come in and phlegmatically pointed to the small heap of his stuff in the corner of the room. It had been rummaged through and beer had been poured all over it, but the important stuff was still there. She said to him, "Too bad, mister. You got Benned", and walked away into the storage room.

Indeed, Big Ben had taken care of him, on request of the crew chief who had radioed down to him the day before. He had described Marko, who clearly wasn't cut out for tree planting, and if he saw him, Big Ben was to make sure that Marko, like all the other pains in the ass, would get the message and leave town. The crew chief only meant for Big Ben to do this verbally because his stature and voice were proven to be enough to get the message across to anybody. But Marko ignored his warning, played it tough and stayed too long, stupidly challenging Big Ben to a game or two of pool.

Yet another mistake. Big Ben was an expert in detecting sharks and being challenged by one always inflamed him to just short of murder.

Marko's Return

For a while, no one knew where Marko was. He didn't call Olena for a stretch of three weeks, during which she worried. She called Robert and Helena to see if they'd heard from him, she called Peter who had moved temporarily to Ottawa for a government finance job, and she even called an RCMP general number to see if they had any reports of a dead man.

Finally one day, Marko called Olena to let her know he was still alive and working in a town called Nelson in southeast British Columbia. Olena didn't know where that was; he might as well have been on the other side of the moon. A few months later, he showed up on Olena's doorstep with a girlfriend. She was the woman that worked behind the bar at Big Ben's. Her name was Elizabeth and from the moment she saw beat-up Marko entering, looking for his pathetic bundle of belongings in the corner, she knew he needed someone.

Olena gave him a big hug and then pulled back to take a good look at him. In the time that he'd been away, he had changed. He explained away the scar on his forehead with a lie about an accident with tree planting equipment. He'd lost some weight and his face was tanned except for the crows-foot lines beside his eyes, lines of white from squinting against the sun. He didn't tell her the lines were from hours on the shoulder of the highway, bumming rides home with pretty Elizabeth whose good looks helped to shorten the wait time between rides.

Elizabeth was lovely, laid-back, and golden-haired. She had fallen for Marko and was determined to save him. She was also quite ready to leave the West and the bar and all the nonsense she witnessed within it. It would be best for them to move on and find a new circumstance before circumstance found them.

Olena was quite taken by Elizabeth and her calming effect on Marko. She had a wry sense of humour and a cute shrug of her shoulders indicating a self-deprecation that served her well. She was the only daughter of an old-money wealthy corporate family from Toronto, but she felt more at home in trappings of less extravagance. Coming into Olena's humble home felt comfortable and Elizabeth was happy to meet Olena to get a deeper glimpse into the man that Marko had yet to fully reveal. She wondered why he had so misplaced himself by venturing West, and wondered if he could fit better near home in the East. It would be up to him to figure it out, but if Elizabeth had more clues, she would be in a better position to nudge him in the right direction.

Peter in Ottawa

From Olena's phone calls, the family learned that Peter had left his job in Ottawa and had moved to Calgary to work for a large, multi-national oil company. He told her that his command of street French was one of his qualifications for managing a crew from Quebec. But in reality he had been quietly let go from his government job when his fiscal shenanigans and utter lack of real qualifications were discovered; let go quietly to avoid bad press and questions about proper controls and oversight. For a while, Peter kept a very low profile. He wanted his mother to think he was good and truthful, and honourably employed. But, tabernac, there never was any crew to manage.

Peter in Banff

Instead of actually going to Calgary, he slipped past and further west, turning up into Banff on a Mountain Lines highway bus. On the main drag, he found a job easily at one of the lodges, which also offered him a little room of his own with a mostly obstructed view of Mt. Rundle. It took him a while to get used to the altitude, which forced him to walk slower and breathe deeper.

In a phone call to Olena, he let slip that he had seen an elk, a bear, and a bighorn all in the same day. That exciting bit of news was relayed by Olena as something normal for downtown Calgary where she thought he was living.

One thing that amazed Peter for a long time was being able to wash his hands and having them go practically dry before he could reach his towel. Isabella would have likened that to going to confession, but it was more like a metaphor for how he had run his life up to that point. That same dry air caused his nose to bleed often, and the altitude made a single pint of beer go straight to his head. The boss he worked for reassured him that he would get used to the beer thing in time, but Peter rather hoped not because his budget was tight. He was already saving money to get back home.

Peter stayed in Banff through the winter and enjoyed working at the lodge because his tasks and responsibilities varied from day to day and his boss turned a blind eye to many things because he didn't own the business. This was good for Peter because he didn't like to be hawked-over, but it wasn't so good for the lodge because it was starting to look run-down and needed some urgent expensive updates in the boiler room, the fuse box, the insulation, and the window seals.

Some days Peter worked the front desk where he answered the phone to take new bookings, or he welcomed guests and helped to solve issues. Other days he did minor maintenance, which made him appreciate Gregory for never complaining about all the things that he and Marko had broken.

He kept the front entryway clean of snow and cigarette butts, and he handled all the cash that came across his desk, some of it making its way into his pocket. He wrote cheques up to the maximum set by the boss, he rolled coins, and he made bank deposits. He learned how to handle the new credit cards that some people were starting to use, and he wondered how they paid off their bills when they didn't have the cash to pay in the first place.

He had learned a big lesson in Ottawa where he had bitten off more than he could chew. It seemed to him that many of the people in his department were faking it, just like he was, but they were just better at it. Peter loved money and he had been running little scams all his life. But the humiliating experience in Ottawa trimmed his feathers and sent him crashing to the ground. His worst fear was that Olena would find out, so he only talked about good things with her on the phone. He was still kicking himself about the bear, bighorn, and elk story that he'd told her. If she thought about it at all, she'd know he was lying about where he really was.

Lodge Guests

The lodge was never boring because the people kept changing. Good guests were worth spoiling a little to get good tips or recommendations. Bad guests were tolerated because they would soon be on their way. Peter learned to handle them diplomatically to soften their anger or disgust, and then he added their name to a long list kept in the office of people who would, from then on, be told that the rooms were full.

One such awful guest was hurling insults in the breakfast room. To George, the coffee was pig-swill, the pancakes were as hard as the plates they were set upon, the eggs had a noxious smell, and where the hell was the Ketchup? Why did the lights keep flickering? What a dump!

This rude, rude man was making a point to embarrass his wife for making reservations at a three-star lodge instead of a four or five star hotel. Later, Peter could hear the man on the lobby telephone, loudly making a reservation at a fancier hotel down the street, one that would better suit his entitlement.

The Ass Man Cometh

When puffed up and ruffled George went upstairs to pack, Peter immediately called ahead to warn René, the hotel manager, of what was coming, a heads-up among friends. His call to René was overheard by George's daughter who was returning from a walk in town. She had refused to have breakfast with him and her mother, preferring a quiet meal at the diner down the street. She knew her father's foul mood would result in something unpleasant and she wanted no part of it.

"That ass man you told your friend about is my dad," she told Peter, adding with a giggle that she was much nicer than him. Peter said he believed her because it would be hard to be worse. He explained that her parents were moving to the other hotel, but she was welcome to stay if she wanted.

Actually, she was thinking about going home to Vancouver a few days early. She had always wanted to take a train through the Rockies and this might be her chance, alone, without hassle or embarrassment. Peter told her that he had a break in half an hour and asked if she'd like to have a coffee with him at the Corner Diner down the road. Even though she had just been there, which Peter didn't know, she agreed to go after she packed up her things and informed her parents of her new plan.

The sidewalks were snow-covered with a layer of ice underneath, so they walked carefully beside each other. Peter had already acclimatized to the altitude but Laurie hadn't yet, so they moved slowly, with Peter carrying Laurie's suitcase the last part of the way. Stamping the snow off their feet at the doorway of the diner, they moved to a booth near the front window, a bright and sunny place with a good view of the quaint buildings across the street.

They seemed to have really hit it off. Peter and Laurie drank their coffees and talked about everything, forgetting about time. She had lived in Vancouver her whole life except for a few months travelling through Europe after university. He explained himself as best he could, leaving out the unappealing details. He told her that his job at the lodge was only temporary and that he had considered moving on to a big city in the late spring when the skiers left town and things got quiet.

By the Window

A taxi drove George and his wife, Linda, to their new hotel, the driver taking care not to slide on the icy streets. Coming to a skidding stop at a red light, Linda glanced to her right and caught sight of Laurie and Peter having a good laugh at their table by the window. She didn't point them out to George, whose snit over the lodge was made worse by his disbelief that his baby had just stood up to him. He would have been angry that she was socializing with staff, but Linda was always happy to see her daughter having a good time. She wished that she could have ditched George for the day so he could unsnit himself and reset to normal. She wished she could buy a train ticket and take an adventure with Laurie. She wished she was already home so she could hide away in her no-men-allowed space, to relax and bring some art to life.

The stoplight turned green and the taxi was about to pull away when the sound of sirens split the air. A fire truck flew through the intersection, with lights and horns ablazing, followed by two RCMP police cars. There was trouble somewhere, but George and Linda didn't care. They were moving on up to a place that they bloody well deserved.

Peter and Laurie looked out the window to see where the trucks were headed. Laurie noticed the moving taxi, edging out carefully into the intersection in case more trucks were on their way. Locking eyes with her mother, who was sitting impassively by the back passenger door, Laurie hoped that Linda hadn't taken her abandonment too hard and that she would find a way to have a good vacation in spite of her ass of a husband.

When a police officer opened the door of the diner to tell everyone to leave in case the fire spread, the acrid smell of smoke immediately filled the air. Peter quickly threw five dollars on the counter near the cash register to pay for their drinks, and he and Laurie left, following the directions of the emergency flag people outside. It was amazing how quickly the public safety personnel arrived, got organized, and minimized the danger for everyone, except possibly themselves.

Peter's Fire

Chance threw accelerant on Peter's plan to leave in the spring. There was no lodge to work at anymore, only the charred carcass of the building brought down by an electrical fire in the basement. With the furnace running almost constantly to keep the drafty place warm, the wooden floors and wall panels were tinder-dry and ready. Too many guests had asked for space heaters to plug into the wall sockets, and too many of them forgot to turn them off when they headed out to the slopes. It didn't take much for the overloaded circuit to spark a fire in the basement, in a place where it could get to roaring before anyone noticed. It didn't take much time for the fire to destroy the entire building, with the small firefighting crew working hard to preserve the buildings nearby.

Luckily, most of the guests were out for the day, the only casualty being an unauthorized cat that had been brought in secretly to one of the rooms. Since no one knew it was there, it was the only creature that died. People returning from skiing late that afternoon were stunned to find that all their belongings were toasted.

Peter's boss was running around looking for someone to blame, when it was his own lack of due care and attention that gave the fire a reason to start. He yelled and waved his arms at Peter, while Laurie looked on in apprehension. Was there going to be a fight?

The boss screeched, "You're fired!" to which Peter replied, "Uh uh, no! The lodge burned down because of you, you lazy bastard. I quit."

The lodge fire was significant enough to be reported in the national newspapers. Olena and Isabella discussed it over cards, Helena mentioned it to Robert, and Elizabeth read the article to Marko. The manager's name was printed, but not

Peter's, so his indirect involvement, and his job and location details remained unknown.

Olena's Circle, 1990

Olena's small circle of people she loved dearly had dwindled. Gregory and Mykola had both died, and Helena had left for Hamilton. Her boys had moved away, seeking larger adventures, and as time went on, there were fewer friends to visit with. Once she retired from work, she had fewer issues to annoy her but also fewer things to occupy her time.

Olena had begun to wonder what she was still doing on Earth, what purpose did she serve? Her family knew her purpose, her calling, but she didn't quite understand how valuable she was.

Thank goodness Isabella and Antonio were still alive and next-floor. Isabella and Olena got into the habit of playing Canasta on Tuesday and Thursday afternoons, the loser paying out a dollar. Playing cards started out as just-for-fun but grew to something more competitive; the single dollar carried like a trophy in the winner's pocket and battled over in the next round.

They would talk and debate during long games, sometimes arguing over news items or religion, trying to throw off each other's concentration. But their rule was that they could never leave angry. At some point in time, they'd picked up a line from an old Borscht-belt comedian that became their own diffuser joke. When one or the other had had enough of the bickering, they would declare, "I don't like your face!" Olena would try timing it for when Isabella had just taken a sip of her coffee. It was so hard to drink and laugh at the same time.

Antonio was still reasonably healthy, but he didn't talk enough to make invigorating company. Occasionally he sat with them and watched them play but never stayed the whole round. Other times, he occupied himself in the kitchen, discovering that he had a passion for cooking and fancied himself head chef at Chez Isabella. He had retired early and lived on a disability pension because of a worn-out hip socket. In truth, it wasn't so bad, but he'd had enough of working. Now he had to remember to look like he was in pain, especially when he was climbing his Montreal stairs, in case the inspector-evaluator returned to spy on the street again.

Sometimes Antonio and Olena would just get in the car and drive out to see the old factory for something to do.

Toronto

Elizabeth eventually moved back to her family home in Toronto, saying goodbye to Marko on the train platform, as a kind of a test to see if he would follow. A few weeks passed, during which she found a new job in a nearby restaurant tavern, to the total disapproval of her parents but to the delight of her grandmother who believed that wealthy, spoiled offspring needed to put some time into working close to the ground.

Returning from her shift, Elizabeth found Marko huddled up on her portico-covered doorstep, staying clear of a line of sight through any windows. He was lucky that everyone was already asleep and that there was no dog in the house anymore that could sniff out his silent presence and sound the canine alarm.

They ended up living together in Bloor West Village in a tiny apartment on the second floor of a walk-up above a deli. Elizabeth's parents never acknowledged this arrangement and made it clear that if she wanted any inheritance, she better not marry Marko. They knew plenty of eligible men who would fit the bill and who would be more acceptable to them and to their friends. But not necessarily acceptable to me, thought Elizabeth.

As it turned out, Marko was prone to disappearing for a few days at a time, and wasn't willing or able to hold a steady, regular job. It wasn't just the job thing, it was his unreliability that caused Elizabeth to rethink her position. Why did she ever think that Marko was the man for her?

Marko's interest in her had obviously waned over time and he was the one to broach the break-up, saying he needed to go back to Montreal where he felt most at home, and anyway, he didn't want to come between her and her parents permanently. She didn't try to hold him back, and she told her parents the partial truth that she was the one who had come to her senses, even though it was he who broke and ran.

Peter on the Move

On the day of the lodge fire, having lost his meager belongings and his job, Peter decided on a whim to head to Vancouver with Laurie, who he had met only that very day. She phoned her parents at their new hotel, speaking to her mother, to tell them that she was fine and unshaken and on her way home. Thank goodness she had packed her belongings and brought her suitcase with her to the diner, expecting to hop on a bus to Jasper where she would connect with the Via Rail train home.

Peter had only the clothes and warm coat and boots that he was wearing and a wallet that was thin, and there was no reason for him to stay in Banff. Laurie had changed her mind about wanting to travel alone and looked forward to having a companion for the three-day journey, and she was quite certain that Peter would leave her after arriving in Vancouver. No strings attached.

Peter stopped at the bank to empty out and close his account; he wouldn't need one in Banff anymore. He took out all the money that he'd been saving to go home. He hadn't yet figured out where home would be.

After buying himself a few clothes and a toothbrush and toothpaste, all stuffed into a small sack, Peter met Laurie at the bus stop. They boarded a Mountain Lines bus to get to Jasper in a few hours to catch a Via Rail train. They could have taken a bus straight from Banff to Vancouver, but they both wanted to be more comfortable in larger seats with more leg room, and in case of bad weather through the Rockies, they were likely safer on a train than in a bus.

The ride north up to Jasper through the valley was breathtaking. The scenery, with snow-covered mountains on either side of the highway, was majestic, jagged, varied, and imposing. Laurie leaned against the window of the bus, cushioning her head with her folded-up coat, to get the best view she could. Having lived near the Coastal mountains her whole life, she was a little desensitized to them, but the Rockies were something else entirely. Neither she nor Peter could get enough of them.

As she dozed off a bit, a depressing thought wiggled its way into her mind. Those mountains and their rocks, any rock actually, had been and will be on the planet forever, but she would eventually have to die and leave. It really didn't seem very fair.

Peter was on the lookout for some wildlife, and eventually they came upon two large Elk near the edge of the forest a safe distance back from the road. The bus driver slowed down and made an announcement saying that even in this part of the world, a roadside sighting was rare. Laurie joked with Peter, figuring the driver told a little fib to make them feel special and lucky. A few cars had pulled over and people with cameras braved the freezing temperatures, as the Elk stood alertly, ready to run in case of danger. Luck can turn into misfortune on a dime.

The bus stopped for a break at a gas station truck stop, where Peter and Laurie got out to stretch their legs. Peter went into the shop to buy a bag of chips and a Coke. As he checked his change, it occurred to him that he always thought the animal on the quarter was a Moose, but it was really an Elk. When they got back on the bus, switching seats so that Peter could get full views, he mentioned this to Laurie who clarified further, that it was a Caribou, not an Elk nor a Moose. Her grandfather was a coin collector and a detail-oriented know-it-all, who passed on random tidbits to her and to anyone whenever he could. And so did she.

Train in the Rockies

After arriving at the Jasper bus depot, which happened to be in the same building as the small train station, Peter and Laurie went to the Via Rail wicket to buy tickets for Vancouver. This was where they learned three important things from the clerk: the first was that train tickets were expensive, the second was that the train to Vancouver only ran twice a week, and the third was that no trains were running at all for at least another week.

There had been a serious snow and rock slide about midway along Moose Lake, some fifty kilometers west of Jasper, and the train that left last night was stuck there with passengers on board. The company was still deciding on the best course of action. It was likely that the train would have to reverse direction and chug back into town so that a clearing crew could get out there and fix the tracks. No one knew how long any of this would take.

So much for being safer on the train, thought Peter. Laurie seemed more concerned with learning that the train only ran through the mountains at night, which defeated her hopes of having a wonderful view. Ever optimistic, she felt that the rock slide was a blessing in disguise, for them at least, not the passengers on board.

Change of Plans

They sat down on two seats jammed among other people whose plans were dashed upon learning about the problems. Everyone was thinking out loud about what to do and how to keep moving. Peter and Laurie considered their options. They could take the bus back to Banff and another bus further to Vancouver. They could stay in Jasper for a while until the train situation got fixed. They could try to hitchhike but would probably freeze to death. They didn't really know what to do, so they didn't do anything for a while.

The train station had a billboard with ads and notices pinned onto it. Peter wandered over to have a look and to kill some time. He glanced over the sheets of paper that blew up gently whenever anyone opened the door. There were the usual ads for hotels and restaurants, Columbia Icefield Glacier excursions, and All-You-Can-Eat diners, but a handwritten note pinned in the bottom right corner caught his eye.

Someone in town needed a person to drive one of his trucks to Vancouver, in effect shipping it there for a lower cost than hauling it by train. This was their ticket! Peter ripped off one of the precut tags containing a phone number and went back to pitch the new idea to Laurie. If they drove starting tomorrow, they could get to Vancouver in two days without pushing it, and they could leave in the morning to catch as many views as daylight would allow.

There was something about Peter, a kindness and a willingness, that Laurie was attracted to. She didn't really know him, except for the few hours they'd already spent together, but her intuition told her that he was safe. She'd been brought up to see the good in people, to understand that most people had good intentions, in spite of what the news broadcasts and newspapers would have you think. But she was also brought up with a strong sense of self, and a keen eye for a lie, for people who were full of shit from a bull. And her gut had told her when to run before, so she knew she could trust it even if she couldn't explain the feeling right away.

The Monster

Within an hour, they had met with the truck owner and struck an agreement that would get Laurie home. This was no ordinary suburban man's truck. This was a monster that was built tough and high. Its four-wheel-drive could push it through any snow, up any mountain, and down any logging road. It had a growl that made it sound mean and when it rolled down any street, people turned their heads to look.

The owner, Jim Bow, was glad to find someone to drive it to Vancouver but after he caught up to it in a few days in his second truck, he still had a problem to work out. And that's when things got even better.

"I'm not sure what I'm gonna do when I get there. I'll have two trucks in the same place. Gotta get the big one up to that new ski place on Vetter Mountain," explained Jim.

"Did you say Vetter?!" asked Laurie, incredulously.

This was crazy. She couldn't believe her luck and neither could Jim. Laurie's parents lived in Point Grey but had a little cabin up at Vetter where Laurie could live. This was exactly where she wanted to go.

Peter and Laurie each took a spin in a large, nearly empty parking lot to get the feel of the monster and its clutch, and to prove to Jim and themselves that they could handle it. The forecast for the next two or three days was, luckily, dry and overcast, so the driving would be relatively easy but they'd still have to be careful in the mountain passes, and if it dipped just below freezing, black ice was the invisible enemy.

They set off a little after dawn, checking the frost report before they left. The powerful vehicle surged forward and ate up the ribbon of highway, reluctantly slowing down behind a row of less confident cars, eagerly flying past them when a passing lane emerged. Driving during daylight afforded the expansive views that Laurie wanted; visibility was clear for miles.

All was calm until a deer suddenly leaped onto the highway. Peter hit the brakes and missed it by only a few feet, as it continued across and into the forest on the other side. With hearts pounding, they hoped that would be the only excitement they experienced along the way.

At the Motel

Peter drove to their first stop in Kamloops where they decided to stay in a small cheap motel to get some rest before tackling the rest of the route. The motel manager asked them to park over on the side instead of in front of their room so that they wouldn't disturb sleeping guests as much when they left in the morning. He had heard the rumbling sound of that engine when they first drove in.

The manager assumed they were married and apologized that the only room left had two twin beds. Knowing how it worked, Peter asked for a discount for the inconvenience. The manager scratched his head, thought for a bit, and then agreed to a lower price. With a stupid grin on his ugly face, he muttered something rude under his breath so that Laurie wouldn't hear, but she did.

The motel room looked like one from the movies where outlaws would hang out. The cinderblock walls were painted white to make the room look bigger, but one wall had rec-room-style wood paneling, an amateur decorator's attempt at making the room look cozy. The carpet was dingy, giving off a smell of cigarette smoke, and the bathroom was small with a toilet that refilled itself when too much water leaked past the flapper. It was only for one night, only for a few hours, and, with the discount, it was pretty cheap. Peter joked that if they found a cockroach, maybe they could angle for some free coffee in the morning.

When Laurie went out to get a few things from the general store down the road, Peter decided he should phone Olena. He hadn't talked to her in a while and he felt he should let her know that he was ok. She was so happy to hear his voice, she didn't even ask him why he called her collect. He told her that he didn't like the job in Calgary or the flatness of the land, and that he was on his way to a town called Vetter in British Columbia that was a developing ski resort. He'd be able to find a good job in one of the new hotels up there.

Always a Mother

Olena gasped and told Peter sternly to be very careful. She had heard on the news about a big fire that burned a hotel in Banff down to the ground. She implored him to check if the hotels in Vetter had sprinkler systems, unlike the hotel in Banff, which apparently had none. He feigned surprise, and assured her that he would, and then he changed the subject, mentioning that he had met a nice girl and it was her idea to go up there. He would call Olena in a few days when they got to Vetter, when their plans became a little clearer.

In For the Night

When he hung up, he thought about what he'd told Olena. He was being a little presumptuous about going all the way to Vetter with Laurie. There was a good chance that she would tell him to get lost once they hit Vancouver. He would have to stay on her good side if he wanted the option, but maybe after two days on the road, they would both want to call it quits and just move on.

Getting a few things from the store was just an excuse for Laurie to have some time alone to think about what was happening. She had absolutely no reason to be alarmed, but what started with a simple conversation over coffee was developing fast into a relationship. Tonight she'd be sharing a room with a man she still hardly knew. This was not the smartest thing to do, so she made a plan. She would pretend to fall asleep, still wearing her clothes, and she'd keep the truck keys next to her in case she had to run away in the night.

Buying some bread and ham slices and two cans of beer, she returned to the room with the escape plan in her mind. But when she got there, Peter had already turned down the covers on her bed, dimmed the lights, and was fast asleep, on his bed that he'd pushed way over to the other side of the room.

Chapter 7

Comings and Goings 1980–2004

Olena's Calls

When Olena's phone was first installed, the cost of a long distance call was very high. But never mind, she felt it was worth it. Olena's calls helped her family keep track of who was where and what they were up to, and when someone in the family called her with information, she would update everyone else. Sometimes she referred to herself as "The BBC".

It wasn't always good news that got passed around, like Helena's death after an unsuccessful operation to fix a heart problem. In Olena's family, whenever a call was bringing bad news, it typically started with, "Hello. It's me. There's been a tragedy." Nice and direct, straight to the point. Luckily, those calls were rare. Most times they started with, "So, I have some news." And over time, as prices dropped, the calls got longer without worrying about the charges.

Marko

"So, I have some news. Marko came back to Montreal. I am so happy."

He stayed with Olena for a while but found that he had outgrown living with his mother. He had very restless feet but very little education with which to anchor them. He couldn't bear to sit still for too long at any boring task, but could plant himself for hours at a Blackjack or Poker table.

Marko's addictive-competitive personality drew him to casinos at night and back into the pool halls during the afternoons. He gambled his way through the rest of his years, trying his hand in Las Vegas and Reno, eventually splitting his time between Atlantic City and Niagara Falls because those cities were closer to home. He always maintained contact with Elizabeth, even if those contacts were spread thin over the years.

Elizabeth

"So, I have some news. Elizabeth has gone back to university."

Elizabeth inherited some money from her grandmother and decided to use it for her university Masters degree. At times, walking around the University of Toronto campus, she felt old. The majority of the students were much younger and far less life-experienced, and it took Elizabeth a while to settle in and find some people who she called her "mini-tribe". Her fellow graduate students were also younger but there were two or three who matched up nicely in dedication and wit.

Elizabeth chose to major in clinical psychology, specializing in gambling addictions, Marko having been the impetus for her thesis. Although she never told him that outright, he knew and joked that he was proud to have helped her become successful.

They remained friends, sometimes not seeing each other for long stretches, but always reconnecting like no time had passed. Elizabeth realized that she'd formed a kind of addiction to him and to knowing she could reach out to him whenever. Over time, she had forged a strong bond with Olena with visits and phone calls, with the Olena who was rather clueless about her son so didn't even see a need to try to help him. He was just a man doing man things, and he loved his mother, and that was enough for her.

Peter

"I have some news. Peter married a woman named Laurie and they live together in a village at Vetter Mountain somewhere in British Columbia."

During the winter, Peter started with a few contracts to plow snow from driveways, the ski hill parking lot, and the shopping area. He really loved driving the big equipment and although he was aiming for a job grooming the slopes, he drifted into working in a lounge at a bar instead. His days watching the bartender at Uncle Nick's turned out to be good training. He liked being able to sleep late most mornings and work in the evenings, when to him, the town seemed most alive. It was like at the lodge in Banff; things were never dull.

There were plenty of visitors from far-flung places coming to earn the bragging rights of skiing a mile high on virgin territory in perfect snow. Many of their most harrowing stories, though, came from the drive up to the mountain village, on the twisty road with poor sightlines and a drop-off on the west side that offered no mercy.

Helena

"There's been a tragedy. Helena never made it through her operation. Poor woman."

The doctor described it coldly to Robert as cardiac arrest, from which she did not recover. He said he was very sorry, but surgery was risky and didn't always work out like on television. He turned on his heel and disappeared from the waiting room, leaving a nurse behind to inform a shattered Robert of the next steps.

Family Tree

Karolina loved making business trips to Montreal where she stayed with Olena instead of booking a hotel room. She preferred the living room sofa to the pull-out couch, with its thin mattress, lumpy coils, and diabolical metal frame. Once she stayed for five whole days, working and going to sales meetings during the day, spending evenings at restaurants, a movie, and a home-cooked meal, all with Olena. Each time she visited, the vestibule door would be flung open and she would be greeted with a hearty hug. Olena's piercing blue eyes would look her over and she'd hustle Karolina over to the dining table for something delicious to eat after a long journey.

The last time Karolina visited, she tried to find out more about her family's history. When she was younger she didn't think about it or care much about it, but as she got older she began to realize that there were fewer people alive who could fill in her blanks.

Broken Branch

Olena seemed a little agitated and Karolina asked her what was wrong. Olena had become more superstitious over time, probably because of discussions with Isabella, and felt that being asked these questions meant that she was close to death. She said she was uncomfortable as the elder, the last old one standing. Karolina wasn't sure what to say to that, so some questions remained unanswered. She hoped she would get a chance sometime later to try again.

As they walked back from a nearby Indian Fusion restaurant, where Olena devoured everything that Karolina's mother would never have touched, Olena suddenly slowed down and realized something for the first time. She remarked, rather pointedly, that actually, she and Karolina were not blood relatives at all. Just as Karolina thought they were at their closest, Olena was starting to find ways to disengage. She hadn't told her yet about the tumour, a slow-growing but ultimately deadly piece of crap in her lung. There were a few things she still had to do before she could no longer step around it as it grew to block her path.

A Trip Back in Time

During a particularly quiet game of Canasta, Isabella asked Olena if she ever thought about going back to her village. The question caught Olena by surprise and her first reaction was simply "Noh". They continued playing and since Olena appeared to be winning, Isabella pressed a little harder to distract her from her game. She said she had always wanted to revisit her origins and to take Antonio with her. Now it was getting too hard to think of travelling and it would be impossible to walk up the steep cobblestone pathways in her town that was built on the side of a hill. It had been a fortified town in the days when it needed to protect itself from foreign invaders. Later it became a toll-collecting town for people wanting to cross the valley. Now it was a ghostified place because most of the young people had moved away and the old people had died. She should have gone when she first thought of it, but it was too late for her now.

Over the last week or two, Isabella coughed little coughs, between sentences, between breaths. Olena asked her if she was ok because she looked a little pale. Isabella insisted that she was fine, but wiped a shine of sweat from her brow. She soon conceded that she might be coming down with something and maybe they should just finish up. She wasn't really able to concentrate on the game anyway, and Olena didn't want to catch any germs from the playing cards that were moving between them. As Olena stood up to leave, she pushed the dollar across the table, saying, "Here, you can have this today. It always makes me feel better."

Will They Come?

As usual, the surprise question, this time about going home, had been deflected. Olena always needed some time to process, to see how she felt, and some time to decide if it was a beneficial suggestion or one best left at the side of the road. As she went about her normal week, the idea of going home grew larger and more fleshed out. She decided to call Marko and Peter to broach the idea of going and of them coming with her.

When Elizabeth and Marko were still living together, she had asked him a few times about his past and his family, but what seemed like reluctance on his part was really just simply a lack of information. He never saw the point of asking about people who were no longer alive and with whom he had no attachment, and Olena and Mykola had been busy and slightly detached from him so the topic never came up. Olena and Mykola had buried the past in a locked chest full of memories and fading mental pictures, concentrating only on moving one foot in front of the other into their futures.

Elizabeth's phone rang. It was Olena looking for Marko. She hadn't heard from him in a while and she wondered if Elizabeth knew where he was.

"You're in luck, he's staying with me for a few days. I'll pass you to him," Elizabeth spoke excitedly, happy to be able to connect mother and son.

"Olena's calling" Elizabeth said, passing the phone to Marko as he walked into the kitchen. She listened to one side of the conversation as Marko listened to what had now become Olena's idea. He said he needed to think about it. He asked if she had talked to Peter about it yet. Olena replied, trying not to sound accusatory, that she had a much better idea of how to reach Peter so yes she had, indeed, already discussed it with him.

When Marko hung up, Elizabeth asked what it was about. Marko took a minute to think and then summarized, "My mother's getting old and she wants to go home before it's too late. She wants me and Peter to come too."

Elizabeth was genuinely glad to hear this and added that she thought it was a great idea. If Marko and Peter went with her, they could find out more about their families and where they were from. Marko shrugged but had already decided to go. After all, Olena had offered to pay for the airline tickets.

Leukemia

It all happened rather quickly. Telltale signs of a cough, fatigue, and fever were not seen as anything deadly. But in the month that Olena was gone, unearthing her roots in the Old Country, Isabella was sliding fast downhill from healthy to dead. Antonio had taken her to the hospital when she was pale, faint, and short of breath, and afterwards he suffered from the guilt and second-guessing of not taking her sooner, even though the doctor assured him that, with acute myeloid leukemia, there was nothing that could have been done.

Isabella had barely enough time to settle with God, her Last Rites were administered to her by a new priest she hardly knew but who she trusted to help her rise up and through St Peter's gate. Over her lifetime she had collected a mental jar of points in case St Peter had any objections to letting her in, and with her constant visits to confession, she had kept her soul clean and ready. Her will had been written after Antonio's two daughters were born and didn't need any revisions, which was a good thing because neither she nor Antonio had time to think about it. She just faded away in a morphine haze with a final, secret, little bump-up from a sympathetic nurse.

In spite of everything, Antonio remembered to pick up Olena and her sons from the airport when they returned, a week after Isabella was buried beside her long-dead husband Pietro. Olena had no clue and innocently asked, "Where's Isabella? Is she feeling better?"

Antonio looked down, shrugged his shoulders dejectedly, and suddenly his face crumpled. He pulled out his large handkerchief and covered his eyes to rub away his tears. The other people waiting in the arrivals area noticed the scene and only thought how sweet it was that Antonio was overcome with joy, not realizing it was quite the opposite.

Olena was in shock the whole ride home. While she was away, visiting her old home, she gave no thought to Isabella's health. Looking back now, the general signs of illness were there, but she had no clue that it would come to this. On the day that Olena left, Isabella had no clue either.

Antonio had been left to deal with everything on his own, but he had proven more than capable by keeping the arrangements simple. He made sure that the priest arrived in plenty of time to administer Last Rites. He held a small private funeral, inviting some cousins, neighbours, and bingo-friend Teodor. Teodor silently apologized to Isabella in case she could now hear his every thought about her, from the past, present, and future.

Antonio's one regret was that he couldn't wait for Olena to get home before burying Isabella because their priest insisted on the usual three-day period. He did, however, slip a deck of cards and a one-dollar loonie under Isabella's hand in the casket before the lid was sealed forever.

Notes for Isabella

There were so many things that Olena wanted to tell Isabella. On the flight home, she excitedly wrote notes, like a shorthand journal, so she wouldn't forget anything. Isabella's suggestion for Olena to go back home was one of the best ideas ever. Olena wanted to tell Isabella how a take-off and landing felt, how the tray came down from the seat in front, how small the airplane bathrooms were, and what Montreal looked like from above, because Isabella had never flown.

She wanted to tell Isabella how her country's landscape had changed over the years, and how she surprised an old friend by knocking on the door of her cottage unannounced, where they had played as children.

She wanted to tell Isabella how she found the old barn still standing on her father's farm, but it was older and greyer, and shuddering against the wind with loose boards flapping. She searched around and miraculously found the old signpost with her father's name carved in it. It was still planted at the side of the road, sun-bleached and faded, leaning over and covered in protective blackberry tendrils.

She wanted to tell Isabella how she recounted, to Marko and Peter, the story of the great swing competition and how her life started with their father that day.

And she wanted to tell Isabella how they had taken a pre-war-built ricketty train to Mykola's home village, now a large town, and then, asking for directions at the station, they ventured further to Julianna's home.

Of all the things that happened, Olena was sure she wouldn't be able to accurately relay how she felt, seeing Mykola's lookalike grandson, Alexander, when he opened the door to Julianna's home. How she watched him over dinner and noticed every similar movement and expression, knowing that both he and Julianna were oblivious to Mykola's genetic gifts.

So she took the notes that she wrote and she added a letter to Isabella, saying all the things she would have told her if she had sat beside her hospital bed taking shifts with Antonio. She put the notes and the letter into a glass jar, screwed on the top, and took it to the cemetery. There was a temporary marker at Isabella's resting place and the earth was still soft and settling after the burial so it was easy to trowel out an elbow-deep hole in which to place the jar, right over where Olena guessed Isabella's heart would be.

Antonio's Girls

Neither Antonio nor his wife wanted to spend money on a lawyer or go against the teachings of their church, and since neither one ever wanted to remarry, they just carried on with separate lives without getting a legal divorce. Nevertheless they remained attached, bound together by two pink ribbons. Two daughters who rarely saw their father. Two daughters who rarely went to bed without wondering about him.

On the occasions when they did meet up with him, he was kind and gentle but very short on words, so no matter how much scarce time they spent with him, they still went to bed wondering.

After Isabella died, so quickly, Antonio was at a loss for what to do. He was left with all her belongings, intermingled with his own. He needed someone who was detached to help him sort things out, someone who wouldn't see a connection or sentimentality in every single thing in their apartment.

Antonio leaned against the dark mahogany dining room sideboard, cradling the green and black ceramic swan that was nothing special to anyone except Isabella. Her friend Lucia had given it to her shortly before dying in a devastating car crash. Lucia had hand-glazed and fired it herself so it wasn't just a gift of a thing, it was also a gift of time.

After the accident, the swan wasn't just a swan anymore. On the neck and left wing, the whorls of Lucia's fingerprints intermingled with Isabella's, the generous giver and the grateful receiver. The swan reminded Isabella of Lucia every day and how much fun they had when they got together.

Each time she saw it on the dining room sideboard.

Each time she lightly dusted it, handling it carefully, mindful of the prints.

Young boy Antonio did not understand Isabella's anger when he accidentally knocked the swan to the floor, cracking its neck. Picking it up in a clumsy rush, he obliterated the prints and, with that, all physical evidence of Lucia's existence. Antonio could not understand Isabella's grief over a stupid ceramic swan that he managed to glue together almost perfectly with only a faint scar showing at the break. Isabella took not one second to explain it to him, instead dismissing him to feel bad and wonder on his own.

He asked his daughters to come and help him, fully expecting them to decline, but they seemed genuinely excited at the prospect of doing something for him, with him. They came to the apartment and walked tentatively down the hallway from the front vestibule, like people walking gingerly over graves in a cemetery.

The girls hadn't been there in a long time because for one reason or another, Isabella always visited them at their home. She liked the change of scenery and the orderly streets and large yards of the suburbs. Most times she took the bus while Antonio was at work but sometimes Antonio drove her. He would walk her to the door, but if he registered a chill from his not-ex-wife, he would hastily hug his girls, kiss them on their foreheads, and slip a purple buck into their hands.

There were heaps of things piled on Isabella's bed and on either side of it on the floor. There were heaps in the dining and living rooms. In the kitchen. In the back bedroom. Years and years of acquisitions and just-in-cases. She rarely threw anything out that seemed like it could come in handy some day. It wasn't hoarding exactly, but it was Isabella's way of appreciating everything she was given or everything she bought.

Antonio had already taken a first cut, setting aside whatever was important to him, and taking many trips to the back alley garbage cans down the creaking, wooden steps inside the fire escape addition.

It served him right for fibbing. His hip problem wasn't exactly as bad as he had claimed to his employers, but after all this climbing, it certainly would be by the time he was done. It really was exhausting and there was still so much to do.

But he was right. His girls felt little attachment to Isabella's stuff and they worked through it quickly, separating items to check with Antonio at their discretion. A few times, they dissolved into hysterics after finding some childhood art piece or old unflattering pictures of themselves that Isabella had treasured as family gold.

As they retrieved stashed candies, chocolates, and tissues from almost every pocket, they were disappointed, jokingly, to find no coins. Soon the heaps became little piles, and from that, they each chose a few items to keep.

The hard part was throwing out the last pile, the distilled essence of Isabella, the best of what she owned but what was of no use to anyone. They wondered if she was watching and getting angry about their choices, but reasoned that if she didn't like it, she should have done this herself.

The predictable result of getting rid of Isabella's things was that now Antonio had more room in his living space, but the unanticipated result was a great opportunity for him.

When he needed his frequent rests, Antonio hovered in the background behind his girls, watching them work together, chatting, deciding, laughing, arguing, and he thought he should remember to compliment their mother on having done a great job raising them. If he had died that day, he would have died knowing that they would be all right.

Olena Leaving

Almost one year after her trip back home, Olena began to experience problems resulting from the tumour in her lung. She was grateful to have Antonio nearby, who checked on her and took her to medical appointments. Olena continued to make phone calls to her family whenever she could, but some days she was in a medicated fog, and some days she didn't want to talk to anyone. The cells of the tumour in her lung had decided to cast themselves around her body and parked themselves in her brain.

Antonio worried. A neighbour at the end of the block had recently died of a brain tumour and the only thing she had in common with Olena was living in the same area. If the water, or the air, or the buildings they lived in were the cause, he would certainly be in the same unfortunate club. Not to mention years of working in the same cigarette-smoking, toxic-belching factory, during a time when environmental factors hadn't become activist-worthy yet.

Antonio came to sit with Olena and read headlines from the newspaper until she indicated she'd like to hear the whole story. While she still could, he would walk with her around the block, steadying her by the hand, leaning against her when her step faltered.

Over time the walks shortened, until at last, they were only from the front door to the sidewalk, and exhausting. Through it all, Olena refused to go to the hospital, her wish being to die at home propped up in a chair facing the warmth and brightness of the south-facing living room window.

Antonio was very unhappy at the whole process of watching someone else's death. Its timing was so uncertain, its effects were far-reaching, and it seemed entirely unfair that the neighbour's dog was put down so that it wouldn't suffer, but a human was left to struggle out to the very end of the plank.

When his mother was dying, Antonio was incredibly sad. The pending loss of his life-giving, life-long partner, strange as that may sound to others, affected him deeply. As a grown man, he tried not to cry so as not to upset Isabella. But with Olena, his distress soared to a higher level. Olena had been part of his life for a long time, since she first enchanted him over bread and real estate negotiations. He had never tried to claim her as his own, he had never said anything to make her feel there was more to it than solid friendship, and neither had she, except once a long time ago. But there was something special between them. Their mutual and unspoken bond was stronger than any vocalized love.

For him, she was like buried treasure.

Like stolen glances.

Like priceless art bought at auction, then held privately and never displayed.

Somehow in Olena's day-to-day decline, she held out hope that she would get through it and get better. Her doctors played on the fence, not wanting to guarantee anything one way or the other and be held accountable. Some days were better than others and fooled her into thinking that she had more time.

She didn't want to upset her boys and she didn't really expect them to uproot themselves permanently, but she was growing more hurt and disappointed that they hadn't read between the lines and showed up before she had to ask.

Antonio knew that her sons' inaction was aiding and abetting her illness. The boys had always frustrated him since they were young. It was now time for them to step up and come home.

As he flipped the pages of Olena's small hand-written directory looking for Marko's number, Antonio's mind reeled. He thought of all the hurtful things he could say to Marko when he answered the phone. But just as Antonio was about to pick up the receiver, and as if on cue, the phone rang. It startled Antonio and his entire speech vanished. On the other end was Marko, finally calling to check on Olena, but instead of getting to talk to her, he got an angry earful, Antonio-style.

"What is wrong with you? Your mother is dying!" he shouted. Slamming the receiver back into its cradle, he thought he saw Olena flinch at his words, but she had only twitched in her sleep. She was sleeping a lot these days and not eating much at all.

When Peter called shortly afterwards, Antonio was ready to pounce once again. But Marko had already sounded the alarm and Peter was just calling to say they were both on their way home.

Chapter 8

Finale
2004

After the Burial

After Olena's burial on that cool and damp late summer Friday afternoon, we milled about in the cemetery parking lot before leaving. I looked around at the small crowd and was able to recognize some people that I remembered meeting at one time or another. I was as old now as they were then.

They had variously come over to Helena and Gregory's or to Olena and Mykola's while we were visiting, all joining in the summer get-together fun. Now funerals seemed to be their big social events.

They shared the common bond of forced emigration, stories of Displaced Persons camps and resettlement, and they sang songs of the old country late into the hot, summer nights. Now they had all aged and changed, and looked at me blankly until I said my name. "Hello, I'm Nicole."

Silently wondering who would be next, this group of friends was getting smaller each year, and not only in number. The men, in particular, were now shorter than I remembered, but I had grown and they had shrunk with age.

A man, who I remembered to be very handsome and charming, was now a bent-over, shaking, underweight suggestion of his former self. He tried to stand a little taller when I introduced myself.

At the recognition of my name, his smile seemed to pull up his shoulders. His wife, standing beside him, reached out and held my hands, and with sunken, cloudy eyes looking straight into mine, told me wistfully that she had loved and dearly missed my father.

I always thought that my father and her husband looked similar. She might have been mixing them up, but I'd heard it before. Several women had said the same, which made me wonder what my father was like as a youth. A romantic, a gentleman, a charismatic playboy? I didn't see that in him, but these women clearly did and strongly enough that they felt they had to say it to me, because even though he was long gone from their lives, and mine, the impression was still strong.

We all piled back into our cars to drive down the mountain, from a beautiful, tranquil, soul-resting place to the urban cacophony of cars and buses, and sirens, and honking, impatient horns.

At the Greek

We all rejoined at a Greek restaurant in the Plateau, to eat even if we didn't feel like eating; to share a toast to Olena even if it cracked our hearts to admit that her death was the reason for our gathering; to sing her favourite songs even if it wasn't appropriate to seem joyful; to pretend that she was with us, for once not cooking and serving up the food.

The older we cousins got, the smaller our age gap seemed to be. Six years difference in youth was like being in another generation, but now we weren't so different anymore.

Marko came over to talk to me like he knew me well, and I, in turn, didn't shrink from his sudden attention. Peter joined us and surprised me with mentioning a few details of my life. My sister, Karolina, asked Peter how he liked living now in Whistler, British Columbia and how his job at the Chateau was going.

Elizabeth, who had driven in from Toronto, asked Peter's wife, Laurie, about her work with Somalian refugees in Ethiopia. Was she planning on going back to the camp where she met the famous "Good Samaritan" Dimitri?

I turned to Elizabeth and asked her how her work with addiction counseling was going. I mentioned, on the hush, that I'd heard she had a high profile case with a local politician, unnamed of course.

We all knew something about each other's lives, not from each other directly but from Olena's calling. We all have a purpose in life, a "calling". Olena's "calling" was calling us.

The Greek owner of the restaurant knew Olena well. She and Isabella came there for dinner about once a month, usually ordering beef moussaka and chicken souvlaki, with Olena calling in advance to secure their table in the warm spot away from the drafty door in winter or the outdoor table in the shade of the oak tree out front.

Olena had hooked Isabella on Demestica on a dare, and Nektarios had a half-litre ready for them each time on arrival. He laughed and joked that they were his favourite customers, although Olena had heard him say that to others as well, but he had a way of making them feel welcome and making them want to come back over and over again. He too mourned the loss of his faithful and predictable customers, and although he wasn't able to attend Olena's funeral, he was proud that his restaurant was chosen for the wake, and he provided everyone with a free shot of Ouzo after their meal.

The Wrap-up

The after-life-party was beginning to wrap up. Several older people had already shuffled out the door, others lingered to talk, and one man surreptitiously threw back any untouched Ouzos left on the tables. This was a generation where nothing went to waste, but that thought nothing of getting completely wasted. He suddenly turned a sickly shade of green and bolted to the back.

Nektarios knew that not everyone would love Ouzo but he was offended at the old man's lack of appreciation and basic theft of a gift that he had planned to pour back into the bottle after everyone left.

Eventually, only the core of the family remained. We were each telling our own stories of what Olena meant to us, and just as Peter was finishing up his version, the restaurant door opened and a man came in, apologizing for being so late.

Marko and Peter both shouted, "Antonio!" and that's when it clicked. The "crying man" at the cemetery was Olena's best friend from the apartment above, from the car on the street, from the factory across town.

I had heard of Antonio, but I hadn't put two and two together at the cemetery because, aside from hiding behind the tree, his cap had been pulled down, his raincoat collar was up, and a huge handkerchief covered his sobbing face.

Antonio excitedly explained his lateness with, "I was at the airport", and added, "Wait. Don't move."

Who Is *That*?

Antonio went out the door and came back a few seconds later, with Julianna and her son right behind him. A roar of surprise rose from our little group, which piqued Nektarios' curiosity. He spied the beautiful older woman, who he hoped would become another long-term customer, and the spitting image of Olena's good-looking husband whom he'd seen in photographs that Olena had shared with him one lonely night, eating alone after Isabella had died.

Julianna's son, Alex, was nearly the same age as Mykola when he died so the resemblance was quite stunning. We all saw it. Even though he was only thirty-eight years old, he had gained a few grey hairs on the sides of his head and in the five o'clock shadow that had sprouted during his long flight over the ocean, making him look older and more distinguished.

Karolina and I had never met Julianna or Alex before. Once, many years ago, through the open window in Robert's bedroom, we'd overheard part of a wrenching conversation between Mykola and Gregory as they swung outside together, Mykola's deep bass carrying further than he realized. We were surprised to hear him getting choked up and we heard him mention Julianna's name, but then his voice dove down to a whisper. Now we sat at our table and watched to see what would happen next.

Karolina whispered to me, "Alex looks like Mykola, doesn't he?" She saw it right away, from her memory of summer visits with Mykola, from the black and white photos in the albums at our house. I was thinking the same thing. I was dying to find out if we were right.

Alex's command of English was excellent. His generation had learned it in school and had more access to media than others before him, so he was very comfortable and his accent wasn't very strong. He explained that the last time Olena called, she told them that she was sick and probably wouldn't have long to live. Her wish was to see them again, but she understood if it would be impossible.

Too Late

Julianna and Alex decided that they would indeed make the trek to Montreal to see Olena, and it was their sincere regret that they hadn't come earlier, before she passed away. A slow death's ending is difficult to time, but with their airline tickets already purchased, there was no point in backing out. They would come and make their best effort to pay tribute to the woman who kept on sending them money each year, taking over from where Mykola left off.

This little detail, about the money, surprised some of us. And there you had it. Alex had mentioned Mykola's name.

As soon as I had a chance, I pulled Marko aside and asked him who these people were and what was going on. He filled me in quickly about Mykola and Danusia, about Julianna's birth and her visit here in 1963, and about Olena visiting them in 2001.

He told me that Olena and Julianna had been in touch for years, first only by mail, then by phone and mail, and that during that brief visit in 1963, Olena had somehow, in her mind, gained a daughter and later a grandchild. It was her way of forgiving Mykola for never having told her his secret until his hand was forced. It was her way of gaining closure for the issues unresolved between them because of his untimely death-by-truck. It was her way of helping out the ones left behind in a country not as wealthy and secure as our own. But she never spoke of the continued contact beyond mentioning it to Marko and Peter. It was her own private gesture, unexposed to the judgment or the opinion of others.

In all the years that we'd been coming to Montreal, we never heard anything about Julianna and Alex, and we heard of but never saw Antonio and his mother Isabella. I could understand not knowing or seeing Julianna and Alex, but how could I not have met Antonio and Isabella? They lived right above Olena in the same building for years, and yet, when we came to visit, they were nowhere to be found. It was quite puzzling to me.

Again I tried to pull Marko aside, but he was busy talking to Nektarios about getting some food for the new arrivals. Nektarios was one step ahead, already planning how to best impress his new customer who had dazzled him with one look. Nektarios was the ever-optimistic, ever-opportunistic restauranteur, and the neighbourhood loved him.

I moved over to where Peter was sitting with Laurie to get the scoop on Antonio. Peter was a little reluctant to talk because Laurie hadn't heard this story yet herself, but he started to explain anyway. It turned out that each time we came to visit, Antonio and Isabella would head into the Laurentians for a vacation in the mountain-fresh air, surrounded by trees and water instead of limestone and asphalt. Olena took time off of work when we came, and so Antonio did too because he didn't have to drive her to the factory. It was as simple as that.

Who Knew?

That explained Antonio and Isabella's absence during our visits, but there was, of course, a lot more to Antonio and Olena's story than that. The neighbours knew, the factory workers knew, the cows in the dairy aisle knew, Antonio's not-ex-wife knew, and the Polish lady knew. Isabella had known, Olena had known, and now we knew too. Karolina and I suddenly understood why Marko and Peter had felt free to leave and lead their own lives. They knew that Olena had a caring, watchful, protective guardian… and they also knew.

Answering the Calling

Julianna and Alex were put up in Olena's apartment during the days that they stayed in Montreal. From her previous visit long ago, Julianna had only a vague recollection of how it looked inside, but a clear memory of the steep, twisted steps outside. We helped Peter and Marko to sort and clean. Karolina, Elizabeth, and I could only stay for two days after the wake at the restaurant, returning home to get back to our jobs. We loosely planned to come back on the next long weekend if work still needed to be done.

But by Wednesday, I was curious to know how things were going.

I picked up my phone.

I tapped in Olena's number.

I became the one.

Marko answered Olena's phone, ringing on Olena's small table with the well-worn matching chair in the dining room corner nook. He turned to the others in the room and with a smile on his otherwise brooding face, he exclaimed,

"Nicole's calling!"

The End

Appendix

Who Are All These People?

My writing is about as far away from Tolstoy and Tolkien as you can get, but the one thing we have in common is including many people in our stories. I've read "writing advice" that encouraged limiting the number of major and minor characters so as not to confuse or overburden the reader, but that to me means limiting the depth of the story and moving it further away from what real life is like. A stranger pulling you back from the crosswalk in time to save your life is as important to you as a long-time family member who you know precisely.

So, I've included plenty of people who make up the little universe of *Olena's Calling*. I couldn't help it. They just wouldn't stay away.

If you skipped to this Appendix before reading the book, you might be the type of person who is curious and likes to meet the cast before the show, or who reads "Trivia and Goofs" in IMDB before seeing a movie.

If you came here after reading the book, I hope you find a few things that clarify or make you want to read the story again.

In any case, I hope you enjoy it.

Characters in the Old Country

Danusia Mykola's first love

Dr. Natas Evila Field doctor, entrepreneur

Ihor Durnay-Pahn Husband of Lilianna Mudra-Baba, trader

Julianna Mykola and Danusia's daughter

Lilianna Mudra-Baba Benevolent benefactor of the Academy

Lubomir Farmer who provides refuge for Mykola

MacAntin the Brute Scottish mercenary warrior

Miss Katerina School administrator, Mykola's friend

Mykola Pronounced Mick-OH-la

Old Dido Mykola's grandfather, son of MacAntin

Olena Mykola's second love, pronounced O-LEH-na

Stefan Mykola's father, son of Old Dido

Taras Danusia's guardian

Characters in Canada

Alex Julianna's son, Mykola's grandson

Allison Intern newspaper reporter

Alphonse/Alpha Olena and Mykola's nasty tenant

Antonio Isabella's son, Olena's friend

Big Ben Enforcer / bouncer

Daria Helena and Gregory's tenant

Elizabeth Marko's girlfriend

George and Linda Laurie's parents

Gregory Helena's husband

Helena Mykola's cousin, Gregory's wife

Isabella Antonio's mother, Olena's best friend

Jim Bow Truck owner

Laurie Peter's friend

Lucia Isabella's long-dead friend

Madame Laflamme Ballet studio owner / instructor

Marko and Peter Mykola and Olena's sons

Nektarios Owner of the Greek restaurant

Nicole and Karolina Robert's daughters,
Helena and Gregory's granddaughters

René Hotel manager

Robert Helena and Gregory's son

Stanley Funeral home director

Teodor Isabella's old bingo friend

Uncle Nick Pool hall gangster

*** Spoiler Alert ***

Insider Information

Pg. 8 "Ugly spawn" refers to the evil twins and Giant Bogdan.

Pg. 8 MacAntin is a reference to my grandfather Antin.

Pg. 9 "Mudra-Baba" means "smart woman".

Pg. 9 "Durnay-Pahn" means "dumb man".

Pg. 10 Giant Bogdan was a short man. His "crazy" made him seem bigger.

Pg. 13 "Sharovary" pants are typically worn by male dancers. The Furies wore them for comfort and practicality when riding horses.

Pg. 15 "Strength, grace, caution, and decisiveness" is the Ukrainian Scouting motto.

Pg. 20 Oy-yoying is the act of exclaiming "Oy yoy!" repeatedly while under condition of surprise or stress.

Pg. 21 "Dido" means grandfather and is pronounced "Dee-doe".

Pg. 32 The twin sisters built up their own reputation and the superstitious villagers were afraid of them. They convinced people that they were capable of casting spells, and myths and legends grew about them. There was no cauldron. There was no wolf meat. The evil twins were not real witches at all.

Pg. 46 'shine refers to moonshine.

Pg. 48 Three bells ringing for six seconds each signaled the funeral of the evil twins, signifying the devil's number 666.

Pg. 55 Old Dido died of pneumonia.

Pg. 57 The name "Lubomir" means "lover of peace". It's a good name for a man who provides refuge.

Pg. 60 Olena was my grandmother's name.

Pg. 68 A Dépanneur is a convenience store.

Pg. 76 Dr. Natas Evila's name spelled backwards is "Satan Alive".

Pg. 84 Daria's Ocelot fur coat signifies that she was going on a hunt for Natas Evila. An Ocelot is a solitary creature, like Daria.

Pg. 88 Reference to six features of six inventions and six future modifications signifies the devil's number 666.

Pg. 95 Highway 2 was a route to Montreal before Highway 401 was completed.

Pg. 99 Gregory grew dahlias and had a thing for Daria.

Pg. 106 Chicago Ride means a fast and furious taxi ride with a fun/crazy driver.

Pg. 116 Lac McTuque (pronounced "Mik-2'k) is a reference to my mother's maiden name "Mykytiuk".

Pg. 122 Antonio's "mental yellow card" is an image of a soccer referee issuing him a "caution" for misconduct.

Pg. 125 It is mentioned that there were eight people for dinner. Don't forget to count the boys.

Pg. 129 "Son-a-fabitch" is the way I would hear my parents say "son of a bitch".

Pg. 130 "Ma très belle maman" means "my very beautiful mom" in French.

Pg. 143 Lubomir got the details of his accident from Stefan afterwards because, of course, Lubomir was unconscious during most of it.

Pg. 152 "Tesoro mio" means "my treasure" in Italian.

Pg. 182 "Tabernac" is a bad swear word in Quebec French. Don't say it.

Pg. 193 The VIA rail train goes through Jasper, not Banff. I checked.

Pg. 198 "Vetter" means "cousin" in Swiss/German.
Mykola and Helena are removed-cousins.
Marko/Peter and Nicole/Karolina are removed-cousins.
Isabella and Antonio have lots of cousins.

Pg. 211 A loonie is a Canadian $1 coin.

Pg. 215 A purple buck – Canadian $10 bills are purple.

Pg. 224 Demestica is a pine resin-infused Greek wine.

Pg. 224 Ouzo is an anise-flavoured Greek aperitif